SERENITY AT SEAGROVE

South Carolina Sunsets, Book 12

CHAPTER 1

The long road stretched out before Luna Mason. It was flanked by the lush greenery that only the South could provide. Giant live oak trees draped with Spanish moss arched over the roadway, creating a tunnel effect of quiet beauty. She rolled her window down, allowing the salty breeze to tease her hair and fill the car with the ocean scent. The air seemed lighter here as if it carried whispers of possibility and new beginnings.

Her hands tightened on the steering wheel as the miles to Seagrove dwindled. She had waited so long for this moment, imagining it repeatedly in her mind. It was a daily visualization she had done for so many years that she couldn't even remember how many it was. But now that she was here, her excitement was tangled up with nervousness, leaving her stomach fluttering with anxiety.

She could still picture herself here as a wide-eyed ten-year-old running along Seagrove's sandy shores during the one and only vacation her family took when she was a child. Her parents hadn't had much, and they had saved a long time to take that one beach vacation. It had been magical, not the kind conjured up by fancy hotels or big amusement parks, but the quieter kind, with bonfires on the beach, looking for perfect pieces of sea glass, with the warm embrace of an island that felt like home from the very moment she had stepped onto it.

Nothing else held her there - no family members, no history. Just that one vacation to Seagrove had been enough to make her long for it for the rest of her life. Her grandmother had loved hearing her childhood stories about Seagrove.

"If it made you that happy, darling, it must be a special place," she had said more than once.

Now, thanks to an unexpected inheritance her grandmother had left her, Luna had finally been able to take the leap that she would have never dared to take otherwise.

Serenity at Seagrove. The name alone filled her with excitement and hope and a healthy dose of apprehension. What if her new business didn't work? What if the dream that she had focused on so carefully, all the way from Austin, Texas, crumbled the moment she saw it in person? Her holistic health center had been designed and built while she had managed everything remotely, balancing blueprints and contracts from all the way in Texas. She had poured every ounce of energy into this venture, leaving her whole life behind because it felt like it no longer fit her.

A psychotherapist in the bustling city, she'd spent her days helping others untangle their lives while quietly mourning her own. When the pieces of her life had fallen apart—her marriage, her plans for a family, her own sense of belonging—she decided it was time to start over completely.

She had adored her grandmother. She was her father's mother, and she had seen her so much throughout her life that she felt like she was a second parent. Losing her had been hard, but her grandmother had given her that one final gift of an inheritance large enough to make her dream come true. Luna had been blessed by wonderful grandmothers on both sides of her family, and she considered herself so lucky because of it. So much wisdom had been passed to her over the years she spent with both of them, and she prayed that wisdom served her well now.

Now here she was, following that faint childhood memory of happiness back to Seagrove. The GPS chirped, pulling her from her thoughts. She looked at the screen—only five miles to go. Her heart rate sped up, a mixture of anticipation and doubt.

Would Serenity be everything she'd imagined? She had chosen every detail with care. The soft coastal hues of the rooms, the deck to do yoga overlooking the ocean, the small garden that she'd dreamed of planting with herbs for teas and tinctures—but she'd yet to see all of it with her own eyes.

She thought of SuAnn from Hotcakes, who'd been a lifeline in the planning of this opening. "You're going to love it here, honey," SuAnn had said in one of their many calls. "Seagrove has a way of welcoming folks just like you."

She'd met SuAnn after calling the local chamber of commerce to get some help with planning. SuAnn had jumped right in, even though she owned a bakery and had no experience with a holistic retreat. She hoped to find more friends like her. The last thing she wanted to feel was like an outsider, like the new girl with big dreams and not enough roots. She needed this place to feel like home to her. She needed the center to be more than just a business, but be a haven for others to heal—and maybe a way to heal herself too.

The first sign for Seagrove appeared, the words painted against a weathered blue background. Her chest tightened. She was almost there.

She slowed as the trees thinned, revealing glimpses of the ocean shimmering off in the distance. A smile broke across her face. She couldn't remember the last time she'd felt this way—hopeful, alive, and ready to embrace whatever came next.

"Well, this is it. No turning back now," Luna whispered to herself. "It's time to live my dream."

The tires of Luna's compact car crunched softly against the gravel driveway as she came to a stop in front of her new home. Her breath caught at the sight before her. Serenity at Seagrove stood proudly in front of the ocean in the midday sunlight. This was a vision that had once only existed in her dreams. All of her sketches and visualizations were brought to life right in front of her. Her chest tightened as a surge of emotion flooded her body—pride, disbelief, and the faintest little bit of fear.

She had painted the house a soft and welcoming shade of pale pink. It looked like it belonged right there on the beach and had been there forever. It was framed by swaying sea oats and dunes that were kissed by the ocean breeze. The outside exuded such charm and warmth, and it was exactly what she wanted her clients to see when they arrived looking for a break from their lives.

White trim outlined the windows, and there was a wide, inviting front porch that wrapped around the front and the sides, complete with rocking chairs that seemed to call to anyone passing by to sit, relax, and lose themselves in the rhythm of the ocean waves. There were some strategically placed potted ferns and blooming flowers brightening up the already sunny facade.

She turned off the engine and sat for a moment, taking it all in. Her hands trembled slightly on the steering wheel, so she pressed her palms flat against her lap to steady herself. After all, she would teach people about stress reduction and how to be healthier in mind, body, and spirit. She had to take her own advice.

"This place is really mine," she whispered to an empty car.

She had poured herself into the design, managing every detail between therapy clients from her small apartment in Austin, Texas. And now here it was, not just an idea in her mind, but something solid and tangible. Finding a lot on the beach in Seagrove was rare, so she was thankful when this one came onto the market. She snatched it up within days of it going up for sale and never looked back.

She pushed open the car door and stepped out into the warm, salty air. She closed her eyes and took a deep breath, remembering that childhood vacation like it was yesterday. Her sandals crunched against the gravel as she moved toward the house, her heart beating faster with each step.

A sign near the entrance read "Serenity at Seagrove." The words were etched in an elegant script on a wooden plaque that she had painted to match the pale pink of the house. Her grandmother's words echoed in her mind.

"If it made you that happy, darling, it must be a special place."

She reached the front porch, placed her hand on the smooth white railing, and ran her fingers along the wood. The porch stretched wide and had plenty of space for morning coffee and afternoon chats. Her gaze shifted to the double front doors, which were flanked by tall windows that allowed sunlight to stream into the house. The soft breeze carried the scent of the ocean, mingling with the faint aroma of the freshly cut wood and paint. The house had just been completed a week or so ago, and she'd made it just in time.

Luna reached into her bag for the key and hesitated momentarily. What if it wasn't everything she'd hoped for? What if the inside didn't match the image she had carefully curated in her mind? She shook her head, shaking away the thoughts. This place was hers, perfect or not, and it was the start of something new.

The key turned quickly in the brand-new lock, and the door swung open with a gentle creak. Cool air greeted her as she stepped inside, and it had the unmistakable smell of a new house. It was one of the reasons why she loved going to home improvement stores—the smell of wood and paint just did something to her, like perfume did for other people.

The space was bright and open, just as she'd imagined. Large windows framed a view of the beach and ocean beyond. The walls were painted a soft cream color, a neutral backdrop that allowed the natural light and the coastal scenery to take center stage.

To the left was a cozy seating area featuring a pale blue sectional and a few accent chairs arranged around a coffee table made of reclaimed driftwood. A bookshelf sat snugly in one corner, stocked with titles that Luna had carefully chosen for her guests— books about mindfulness, healing, and finding balance. The floors were wide planks of light oak that gleamed underneath her feet.

To the right was an open kitchen with white cabinets and quartz countertops with a backsplash of soft green tiles that brought in the ocean beyond. They looked like pieces of sea glass gleaming in the sunlight. A large farmhouse sink sat underneath the window that overlooked the dunes. Luna imagined herself standing there preparing meals for guests or washing dishes while watching the waves roll in. The island in the center of the kitchen featured seating for three—a place where guests could gather for tea or quiet conversation.

She walked deeper into the house, her sandals silent against the oak floors. The three guest rooms lined the hall to the left, each with its own ensuite bathroom. Luna peeked in the first room, smiling at her chosen touches. It was painted a pale aqua, the color of the sea on a sunny day. A queen-sized bed with a white linen duvet and a woven throw blanket sat beneath the window that framed the dunes. A small desk and chair and a vase of fresh flowers completed the space.

The other two rooms followed a similar design, each with its own subtle theme inspired by the beach. One was a coral-accented room, while the other featured sandy tones with pops of navy blue. Each room felt like a haven—a place where someone could find rest and renewal—which was precisely what Luna had intended. She would be able to house three guests at a time, and she hoped to be full as much as possible so that people could help each other while she was helping all of them.

A set of double doors opened to the yoga deck at the end of the hall. The view here took her breath away. It stretched toward the dunes with enough space for small classes to practice while listening to the soothing sound of the waves. There was a pergola to provide shade, and fairy lights were strung along the beams. She couldn't wait to see it at nighttime.

Her personal quarters were tucked in the back of the house and offered her a private retreat. She loved to help people, but at the end of the day, she needed her own time and space. The small but functional living space included a bedroom, a compact kitchen, and a cozy sitting area that opened onto her own private deck. It was more than she'd ever allowed herself to dream of—a home and a sanctuary all in one.

She stepped out onto her deck and leaned against the railing, her eyes scanning the horizon where the sky met the sea. A flock of seagulls flew overhead, their cries mixing with the sound of the surf. The breeze pulled at her long dark hair, and Luna felt a sense of rightness settle over her for the first time in a long time.

This was where she was meant to be.

"Welcome home," she whispered to herself, her voice carried away by the wind. Serenity at Seagrove wasn't just a dream anymore—it was hers.

A rcher Hawk drove his beat-up black truck down the winding road leading to his friend Dawson's inn, a low hum emanating from his engine against the backdrop of the crashing waves. The sight of Seagrove's familiar streets stirred something inside him—not quite nostalgia, but maybe the ghost of it. The town had hardly changed in the years since he'd left. The same pastel storefronts lined the main street and stretched around the square, their awnings fluttering in the Lowcountry breeze. The same clusters of locals lingered on porches or beneath shade trees, talking like time wasn't chasing them down.

Even though he'd been there for much of his life, Archer suddenly felt like a stranger. As he passed the old diner on the corner, a memory surfaced. He and Dawson, scrawny teenage boys at the time, had spent so many summer afternoons here, splitting greasy hamburgers and plotting their next grand adventure or talking about the prettiest girl at school. Dawson had always been the dreamer, talking about the business he'd someday build. At the same time, Archer had been more focused—laser-focused, actually—on getting out of Seagrove and making something of himself. Back then, it all had seemed so simple.

The basketball court by the park came into view,

and another flash of his past tugged at him. He could almost hear the echo of the ball against the asphalt. Dawson's trash talk as Archer inevitably dominated every single game. They'd been competitive with each other, but inseparable—two kids with different visions of the future, but an unbreakable bond.

The sight of the inn up ahead brought him back to the present. It had cheerful blue shutters and neatly trimmed hedges that looked just like he remembered. Dawson had always been meticulous, just like his grandmother, whether it was his work as a contractor or running the inn. The home had been in their family for generations, and it sat right on the beach with a beautiful view. Archer had to admit, begrudgingly, that his childhood friend had built something special here, and as much as he had tried to avoid this visit, it wasn't like he had anywhere else to go.

He parked his truck and climbed out, stretching his legs and wincing as his shoulder protested any movement. The injury had been months ago, but the dull ache always served as a constant reminder of what he'd lost. Golfing had been his life—no, it had been his identity—and without it, who was he? Before he could spiral too far into self-pity, which was where he regularly hung out, the inn's front door swung open. Dawson stepped out, his grin as wide as a summer day. He looked much the same, with his dirty blonde hair sprinkled with bits of gold, and always a little too long for Archer's liking.

"Well, look what the tide dragged in," Dawson called, striding down the porch steps. Dawson had a particular walk, more of a swagger. He'd walked that way as long as Archer had known him, and the girls adored him in school because of it.

Archer managed a half-smile, shoving his hands into his jean pockets. "Figured you need somebody to keep you humble, so here I am. You're still way too good-looking, by the way. It's kind of sickening."

Dawson laughed and pulled him into a quick firm hug that Archer tolerated with a grunt. "You've been missed, man. Come on in. This town hasn't been the same without you."

"Oh, don't go getting too sentimental on me," Archer said, as he followed Dawson up the steps.

Inside, the inn smelled like fresh flowers and lemon polish. It reminded him of Dawson's grandmother. She was such a wonderful woman and always provided Sunday dinner when Archer visited their house. He remembered when Lucy would cook her famous pot roast and when Dawson's granny would make her famous chicken pot pie. His mouth watered thinking about it. The wide foyer opened into a sitting area where a couple of guests sat chatting over glasses of iced sweet tea.

Dawson's wife, Julie, appeared in the hallway, her

arms full of towels. "Archer," she said, her face lighting up. "It's so good to finally meet you. Dawson has told me so much about you."

Archer tipped his head in her direction. "Hey, Julie. Looks like you've been keeping Dawson out of trouble."

"Well, that's a full-time job," she said, winking as she disappeared toward the laundry room.

Dawson motioned Archer toward the check-in counter, where a set of keys waited. "Your room's upstairs, the same one you used to crash in during summer. I figured you'd like something familiar."

Archer hesitated, looking around. The inn was warm and inviting, the kind of place that should make someone feel at ease, but he couldn't shake the tension that always stayed coiled in his chest like a rattlesnake ready to strike. His shoulders hadn't descended from his ears since his injury.

"Thanks, I appreciate it," he said.

Dawson studied him for a moment. "You doing okay?"

"Yeah, I'm fine," Archer said, taking the keys and heading to the stairs before Dawson could press any further. *Fine.* That word had become his shield, a way to deflect everybody's concern and keep people at arm's length.

The room was exactly how he remembered it, down to the worn patch on the braided rug near the window. He set his bag on the bed and moved toward that window, pushing it open to let in the ocean breeze. He'd been back in Seagrove for about twenty minutes, but he already felt the weight of everyone's expectations pressing on him. Hometown hero, the guy who'd gone out and made it big. People loved a success story, but what about when that story fell apart?

He could hear voices on the porch below as he leaned against the window frame. He watched Dawson chat with a couple of guests. He'd always been the friendly one, the guy who could talk to anybody and make them feel like they mattered. Archer had a sharper personality with edges that were hard rather than smooth. It wasn't that he was unkind, at least he hoped people didn't feel that way, but he'd never been the life of the party or the easy-going one. And now with his career gone and nothing to show for it, he felt even more out of place.

His phone buzzed in his pocket, and he pulled it out and looked at the screen. Another message from his agent asking when he was coming back. He ignored it, tossing the phone face down on the bed. He didn't have an answer. Atlanta didn't feel like a home anymore, but neither did anywhere else. Home had been his golf bag. Home had been the green, any green. It didn't matter where it was, but today he was here in his hometown and that had to be good enough for now.

He straightened, rolling his shoulders as he moved toward the door. If Dawson and Julie were nice enough to open their home to him, the least he could do was make an effort to be pleasant. He wasn't here to wallow like he'd been doing for months—well, not entirely anyway. Maybe if he played his cards right, he could figure out his next step, and he didn't have much choice but to try.

CHAPTER 2

Luna stepped out onto the wide porch at Serenity at Seagrove, the early morning sun beating down on her as she stared out over the beautiful South Carolina coastline. This moment was pure bliss. It was everything she'd dreamed about since she was a little girl, and the only thing that would've made it better was having both of her grandmothers there to share in it. Today was a huge day. After months of phone calls, meticulous planning, and emails back and forth, she was finally meeting Janine in person.

Luna had spoken to Janine several times while organizing the wellness center's grand opening, and the yoga instructor's warmth and energy had been infectious. If her phone conversations were anything to go by, Janine being involved with Serenity would be a perfect fit.

The sound of sandals clicking against the steps caught Luna's attention. She turned to see Janine approaching, her curly hair pulled back in a ponytail, and a yoga mat tucked under her arm. She was dressed in a breezy white tank top and pink leggings with a subtle floral pattern, radiating confidence and ease.

"Luna!" Janine called out with a bright smile.

"That's me," Luna said, stepping forward to greet her. "It's so great to finally meet you in person, Janine," she said, shaking her hand.

"Same here. I've been looking forward to this so much. It's not often that I find people in this town who care as much about holistic health as I do, and this place is absolutely stunning. I've so enjoyed watching it be built from the ground up. The pink color is so charming." Janine looked over the house and then back at Luna. "You know, it's got such a welcoming vibe. I can already tell this will be a great place for your guests."

"Thank you," Luna said. Compliments about Serenity felt deeply personal. "And I appreciate all your help watching over the project until I could get here. Come on inside. I'll give you a grand tour."

Inside, Luna led Janine through the main living area, pointing out the seating arrangements, the small but well-stocked library, and the kitchen with the ocean-facing window. Janine took it all in with a mix of admiration and excitement.

"This is perfect," Janine said. She looked out over the yoga deck that opened onto the dunes. "You know, I can already imagine morning classes out here with the sound of the waves as our soundtrack, and evening sessions with those lights. It's just going to feel like another world," Janine said.

"That's exactly what I was going for," Luna said. "You know, a place where people can escape and feel whole again."

Janine nodded. "It's a beautiful goal, and it's so needed today. Some people just need to breathe, you know. This is the perfect place for that. Seagrove itself is the perfect place for that, but this takes it to the next level."

They walked outside and settled onto the deck chairs to go over logistics. Janine opened a neatly organized folder filled with laminated schedules and notes.

"So I thought we could start with three weekly sessions just to get things rolling. Morning yoga at sunrise, an evening wind-down class twice a week. Does that align with your vision?"

"That sounds perfect," Luna agreed. "I want to ease into things, and once we see how the first classes go and how many guests I get, we can build from there."

They discussed themes for the classes, ideas for meditation add-ons, and a way to incorporate the natural beauty of Seagrove into their practices. The conversation with Janine flowed so easily, and Luna felt like they'd known each other for years instead of just weeks.

When they wrapped up the meeting, a voice called from the front of the house.

"Janine, I thought I'd find you here."

Luna looked up to see a woman with wavy blonde hair and a welcoming smile walking toward them. She wore a simple sundress and carried a canvas tote bag that read *Down Yonder Bookstore.* The resemblance to Janine was subtle but unmistakable.

"Julie," Janine said, standing up. "You're just in time to meet my new friend, Luna. This is her amazing place that will change lives in Seagrove."

Julie turned her smile to Luna and reached out a hand. "Hey, I'm Julie, Janine's sister. I own the book-store in town."

"Don't let her fool you. Julie is also a famous romance author."

Julie waved her hand and laughed. "My sister is overstating that a bit. I am an author, but famous I am not."

"Oh wow, it's so nice to meet you," Luna said,

shaking her hand. "I've heard great things about your bookstore. SuAnn mentioned it when we were planning the grand opening."

"Oh, SuAnn," Julie said with a laugh. "She's our local networker. I think she might be responsible for half the friendships in this town."

Janine laughed. "Yeah, she's also responsible for all of the dessert orders at Hotcakes. She owns the bakery, as you know, but she's also our mother."

Luna stared at them. "SuAnn's your mother? How did I not know that?"

Julie chuckled. "Well, it's probably because she didn't tell you. Sometimes I wonder if we embarrass her or something."

Julie looked at the house. "I love what you've done here. Dawson and I own the inn just up the road, so if you ever need a good recommendation for something or a place to put overflow guests, just let us know. We're always happy to help. Dawson also does some contracting work and can build anything, so if you need that kind of help just reach out."

"That's very kind of you," Luna said. "Thank you. It's been a bit overwhelming moving here. I only visited here once as a kid, though I'd always dreamed of coming back. Everybody has been very welcoming so far."

"Well, that's Seagrove for you," Julie said. "Once you're here, you're family."

They chatted for a while longer, and Luna felt increasingly at ease. Julie talked about the inn, some funny mishaps with guests, and heartfelt moments that had made the business more than just a job.

When Janine and Julie left, promising to return soon, Luna lingered on the yoga deck for a moment, the sound of the waves filling the silence. Meeting Janine had been such a gift, and now she also knew Julie. For the first time since stepping foot in Seagrove, she felt the hope that this new chapter of her life might be everything she had ever dreamed it could be.

The hum of the lunchtime crowd at the local café buzzed pleasantly in the background as Luna stepped onto the outdoor patio, the scent of coffee and fresh pastries mingling with the salty air from the nearby ocean. Small black wrought iron tables dotted the space, shaded by large umbrellas that swayed gently in the breeze. She was about to settle into a table in the corner when she spotted a familiar face waving her over.

Julie, with her blonde hair pulled back, sat at a table near the edge of the patio, a canvas tote bag

from Down Yonder Bookstore propped up beside
her chair. She had a half-eaten sandwich and a glass
of sweet tea in front of her.

"Luna!" Julie called, motioning to the empty chair
across from her. "Please join me. You're just in time
for some Lowcountry sunshine and good company, I
hope."

Luna smiled and made her way over. She'd met
Julie just days ago, but her warmth and friendliness
had made a big impression. It had been a long time
since she'd had friends. Back in Austin, she was
consumed with her work and taking on everyone
else's problems. Being alone in the world was hard.
Luna had lost both of her parents before she gradu-
ated from high school. Her father died in a work
accident when she was thirteen, and her mother of
cancer when she was three months shy of graduating
from high school.

"Are you sure? I don't want to interrupt your
break."

"Oh, not at all," Julie said, waving her hand. "I was
just thinking how lunch always tastes better with
company. Please, sit."

Luna smiled and pulled out her chair, setting her
bag beside her. "Thanks. This is a great spot for
people-watching. The view of the square is amazing.
I love all the moss on the trees."

"One of my favorite places to sit in town," Julie

said. "Have you been over to the marsh yet? It's especially beautiful this time of year."

"I'm going to go over there today. I want to take some photos, maybe have them printed to hang on the walls of Serenity."

"How is Serenity coming along? Are you settling in okay?"

"I'm getting there," Luna said. "It just still feels so surreal sometimes. But I'm starting to get my footing. I can't wait to officially open. Janine has been so much help, and I think the yoga classes are really going to help my clients so much."

"That's wonderful to hear. I'm not surprised about Janine. She's just got that gift for connecting with people. Your center is going to be the talk of Seagrove and probably the whole Southeast before long."

Luna chuckled. "Well, let's hope so."

The door to the café opened, and a tall, broad-shouldered man stepped out, his dark brown hair ruffled by the breeze. Luna immediately noticed how he favored his left shoulder, his movements deliberate but careful. He looked around the patio area, his eyes narrowing slightly when he spotted Julie.

"Archer, there you are. I wondered if you'd make it," she said, waving him over.

He approached, and Luna felt an inexplicable tug

of curiosity. His chiseled features carried a weariness that belied the physical strength he obviously had. Despite his brooding demeanor, there was something very magnetic about him. He reached their table, and Julie nodded toward Luna.

"Archer, this is Luna Mason," Julie said. "She's the one who's opening Serenity at Seagrove. It's a holistic healing center. Luna, this is Archer Hawk, an old friend of my husband's."

Luna turned sideways and reached out her hand, but Archer hesitated briefly before shaking it. His grip was firm but not overly so, and his hand felt warm against hers.

"Nice to meet you," Luna said, keeping her tone light despite the look in his eyes.

"You too," he said, his voice deep and slightly gruff.

Julie gestured to the other empty chair beside her. "Sit down and join us. You could use a good meal."

Archer hesitated and then shrugged. "Sure, why not?" He lowered himself into the chair and glanced at the menu Julie slid across to him. He scanned the options as Julie turned back to Luna.

"So I was just asking Luna how things are going with her new business. She's got big plans for the place. Therapy, yoga, mindfulness workshops. Doesn't that sound amazing?"

Archer raised an eyebrow, putting the menu back on the table in front of him. "Yoga and mindfulness, huh? Sounds like a lot of woo-woo stuff to me."

Luna's smile faltered. "It's actually a lot more than that. I'm a licensed therapist, so the center will offer counseling and wellness programs. It's about creating a space where people can reset their lives and take care of themselves."

Archer leaned back slightly, his gaze steady on hers. "Sounds nice for vacationers, but I'm not sure how much real people need that."

Luna's cheeks felt warm, and she tried to mask her irritation. "You'd be surprised. Life has a way of throwing things at you that you can't handle by yourself, and sometimes people need a place to heal."

Julie glanced between them, her expression a mix of concern and amusement. "Archer, you'd benefit from Serenity more than most people I know."

He snorted softly. "Yeah, I think I'll stick to my physical therapy with an actual doctor, but thanks."

Tension hung in the air for a moment before he stood up, his chair scraping against the sidewalk. "You know, I'm gonna go stretch my legs by the marsh. Nice meeting you, Luna."

Without waiting for a response, he strode away, his posture rigid.

Luna watched him go before turning back to Julie, who sighed and shook her head. "I'm so sorry about that. Archer's, well, he's going through a rough patch."

"What happened?"

Julie hesitated. "Well, he was a professional golfer. A shoulder injury ended his career recently, and golf was everything to him. So now he's trying to figure out what's next and who he is without golf. It hasn't been easy for him, needless to say."

Luna nodded. She'd seen pain like this before, the kind that came when someone's identity was ripped away. "Well, that explains the chip on his shoulder," she said. "No pun intended."

Julie smiled faintly. "He's a good guy underneath it all. Dawson's told me all kinds of stories. They grew up together. It'll just take some time for him to find his footing again."

Luna's gaze drifted towards the marsh where Archer had disappeared. Something about him intrigued her despite his rough edges. "Maybe," she said, "but he might need some help that a physical therapist can't give."

⁓

Archer leaned back in the Adirondack chair on Dawson's porch with a glass of sweet tea in his hand. The faint crash of waves in the distance set the stage for relaxation, but Archer rarely relaxed these days. It was a picturesque evening, the kind that would make most people feel calm, but not Archer. His jaw tightened as he stared out at the dusky horizon, his mind a mess of frustration and disappointment.

"You're awfully quiet," Dawson said, sitting in the chair beside him. Dawson, who always had an easy-going charm, looked at home here, like he belonged to the land, the sea, and the community in a way that Archer never could.

"I'm just thinking," Archer muttered, swirling the tea around in his glass.

"That's dangerous if we do too much of it," Dawson said. "What's on your mind?"

Archer's grip tightened on the glass. He didn't say anything for a moment, but then the words seemed to come tumbling out, sharp and bitter. "You ever have everything you've worked for, everything you've dreamed about, just ripped out from under you, just like that?" He snapped his fingers for emphasis.

Dawson didn't respond at first, letting the question hang in the humid air. "Not in the way you have, but I've lost things that mattered. I've had to start over."

"Starting over, that's what everybody keeps saying. *You'll figure it out, Archer, you're young, you've got time.*" Archer scoffed. "You know what I had planned? I had the next ten years mapped out. Tournaments, majors, wins. I was gonna make history, maybe even get my name on a clubhouse somewhere, and now I can barely swing the dang club without this shoulder screaming at me. I'm in my forties with no idea what to do with the rest of my life."

Dawson's expression stayed steady. "What about other options? Mentoring golfers? Coaching pros? You've got experience. That's something a lot of other players could learn from."

Archer shook his head. "I don't want to coach. I don't want to be a commentator or some talking head on TV. I want to *play*. That was my plan, Dawson. That was *the* plan."

Dawson leaned back, crossing his arms over his chest. "And now the plan changed. It happens to everybody, Archer. Life doesn't always follow the script we write, and at some point, age was going to catch up with you anyway."

Archer finally looked at him. "That's easy for you to say. You've got *this*." He gestured around the porch, the inn's soft glow inside spilling out onto the lawn. "You've built a life. You've got roots, family, and purpose. What do I have? A bum shoulder and a bunch of trophies that don't mean anything anymore. People are already forgetting about me."

"You've got a lot more than that," Dawson said. "You just can't see it yet."

Before they could continue, Dylan came bounding out the front door. "Dad, can I go meet Jason down by the water? He saw some crazy looking crab and wants to show it to me!"

Dawson laughed. "Yeah, buddy. Have fun, but get home before it gets too dark, okay?"

"Woohoo!" Dylan yelled as he ran toward the beach.

"That kid is always at one-hundred or sound asleep. I wish I had his energy," Dawson said, watching as he disappeared down the beach.

"See? You have it all, man. I have no career, no wife, no kids. How did I end up here?"

"There's a plan, Archer. You have to believe that. We can't always choose our path, but we have to trust that we'll get to the right destination in the end."

Archer huffed out a breath and set his glass on the small table between them. "You sound like one of those self-help books that Julie probably has in the bookstore."

Dawson chuckled. "Maybe I've been married to her a little too long. But she's not wrong about those books. And she's not wrong about something else either."

"Oh yeah? What's that?"

"There's that new wellness center here in town, Serenity at Seagrove. Julie's been raving about it since she met the owner, Luna. It's not just about meditation and yoga, though those probably would do you some good." Dawson raised an eyebrow, daring Archer to argue with him. "She's a therapist. The real deal. It might be worth your time to check it out."

Archer scoffed immediately. "Therapy? Yoga? Meditation? Come on, man, you gotta be kidding me."

"I'm not," Dawson said. "I've known you a long time, and I know you're not the kind of guy who likes sitting still, but maybe that's what you need right now. A chance to clear your head and figure out what comes next. Finally deal with those emotions and the thoughts driving you crazy. They need to get out of that hard coconut of yours." He reached over and knocked his knuckles against Archer's head.

Archer stood abruptly, pacing the edge of the porch. He looked out at the darkening sky, his hands on his hips. "I don't need somebody to hold my hand and tell me it's all gonna be okay."

"No one's saying that," Dawson replied, "but you're carrying a lot right now. Maybe it's time to let some of it go."

Archer didn't respond. All he could hear was the

gentle rustling of trees and waves breaking against the shore.

Dawson stood and joined him at the porch rail. "Look, I'm not trying to push you into anything you don't want to do, but you came back to Seagrove for a reason. Maybe this is part of it. Just give it some thought."

Archer glanced at him, his jaw tight. "I'll think about it."

"That's all I'm asking," Dawson said, holding up his hands. He gently clapped Archer on the back. "Now come on, let's grab another glass of tea and talk about something other than golf for a while."

The tension in Archer's shoulders eased just slightly. "Yeah, I think I could use the distraction."

CHAPTER 3

Luna stood in the middle of Down Yonder Bookstore, breathing in the comforting scent of books and the fresh coffee from the small café in the corner. She'd come in looking for some new meditation books to put on the coffee table at Serenity, but found herself lingering. She was always drawn into the cozy atmospheres of bookstores.

"Well, darling, you look like you could use a cup of coffee," came a voice from behind her.

Luna turned to find an older woman with the most perfectly coiffed platinum blonde hair and bright red lipstick, watching her with knowing eyes. She was wearing a flowing pink caftan and multiple silver bangles that jingled when she moved. Her nails were painted in a matching hot pink.

"I'm Dixie," the woman said, extending her manicured hand. "You must be Luna. Julie's been telling me all about you and your new center."

Luna shook her hand. "It's nice to meet you. Julie mentioned you were her partner here at the bookstore."

"Her partner, her best friend, her resident wise old woman. I wear many hats," Dixie said with a wink. "Come on in. Have a seat over here in the café. I've got a fresh pot of coffee and some books I think might interest you. I figured you might come in at some point so I put a few aside."

Luna walked over to the café and sat down. Potted plants filled every available surface in the corners, and a large macramé piece hung on one wall.

"Have a seat, honey," Dixie said, gesturing to one of the chairs. She walked behind the counter and poured two cups of coffee. "Now tell me how you're settling into Seagrove, and don't give me that 'everything's fine' nonsense. I've been around this earth long enough to know when somebody's got some weight on their shoulders."

Luna accepted the coffee gratefully, wrapping her hands around the warm mug. "Is it that obvious?"

"Well, only to those who know what to look for," Dixie said, sitting in the chair across from her. "Opening a new business is never easy, especially one in a small town where you're the newcomer. But I have a feeling there's more to it than that."

Luna took a sip of her coffee. "I guess I'm just questioning a lot of things. Did I make the right choice coming here? Will people actually want what I'm offering? I met somebody yesterday who basically dismissed everything I do as, and I quote, 'woo-woo' stuff." She did air quotes for dramatic effect.

Dixie's eyes opened wide. "Would that someone happen to be a tall, brooding former golfer with a chip on his shoulder the size of Texas?"

Luna's eyes widened. "So you know Archer."

"Oh, honey, in Seagrove, everybody knows everybody, and I've known that boy his whole life." She shook her head. "He's carrying around more pain than he knows what to do with, and he's never been very good at his emotions. Don't take his words personally. He's just lashing out because he's hurting."

Luna shifted in her chair. "I get that he's hurting. As a therapist, I can see the pain written all over him, but I also can't help people who don't want to be helped."

"Well, now that's where you're wrong, sugar," Dixie said, leaning forward in her chair, her bangles clinking against the metal bistro table. "Often the ones who fight the hardest against getting help are the ones who need it most, and sometimes help will come in the most unexpected ways."

Luna raised an eyebrow. "What do you mean?"

"Well, take this bookstore, for example. People come in here thinking they're just buying books, but they end up finding a lot more. Community, friendship, sometimes a listening ear. I imagine it's what bartenders and hairdressers feel like," she laughed. "Julie and I have seen more healing happen between these shelves than most people would believe."

"That's very beautiful," Luna said softly.

"And your place, Serenity, well, it's going to do the same thing. You're not just offering yoga classes and therapy sessions. You're creating a safe harbor for people who need one." She reached over and patted Luna's hand. "Even stubborn ex-golfers who think they're too tough for woo-woo stuff."

Luna couldn't help but laugh. "You seem awfully sure about that."

"Oh, I've been in this town long enough to know how things work. People like Archer, well, they just need to come to things in their own time. But you mark my words, that man's going to find his way to your door eventually."

"Maybe," Luna said, though she still wasn't convinced. "But right now, I just have to focus on getting Serenity up and running so I can help the people who *do* want help. And speaking of which, I should probably look at those books you mentioned."

"Oh, of course, honey," Dixie stood and moved to a shelf behind the counter. "I pulled these aside when Julie told me about your center. I knew exactly who you were when you walked in the door."

"How did you know that?" Luna asked.

"Well, she told me you were a beautiful woman with very long black hair, and that's what stood out as soon as you walked in. I sure wish my hair would grow that long, although I'd look pretty silly at my age."

Luna chuckled. "I think anybody can be anything at any age."

Dixie nodded. "You're right. Well, anyway, there's some wonderful stuff about meditation and mindfulness, and I also pulled a couple of local books—I thought some of our history might interest you."

As Dixie showed her the books, Luna felt some of her earlier tension melt away. There was just something about Dixie's presence that made her feel like this might be manageable, like all of the pieces would eventually fall into place if she just gave them time.

"Thank you so much, Dixie," Luna said as she gathered the stack of books. "Not just for these, but for the talk. I needed it more than I realized."

"Well, that's what we do here in Seagrove," Dixie

said, smiling. "We look after one another, and honey, you're one of us now, whether you realize it or not. We aren't going to leave you alone."

Luna wondered if maybe this was what it felt like to really come home—to find a community that welcomed you with open arms, even when you weren't sure you belonged. As she left the bookstore, her arms full of books, she felt a little lighter. She couldn't help but think about what Dixie had said about Archer. Maybe he would find his way to Serenity eventually, and maybe she'd be ready when he did.

Archer walked along the beach, his feet sinking into the cool sand with each step. The early morning air was thick with salt and humidity, as it often was in the South Carolina Lowcountry. He'd grown up with it, so he barely noticed it anymore. These dawn walks had become his morning routine since arriving in Seagrove a few days ago. They were a poor substitute for the hours he spent on the golf course before his injury, but he needed something to fill the endless stretch of empty days.

His shoulder always ached, a constant reminder of everything he'd lost. The doctors had told him the injury wasn't career-ending, that maybe with a long rehabilitation process, he could return to golf, but probably never at the level he was. But he knew better. He felt as if his entire being had fundamentally broken that day. His spirit was gone.

He knew there were lots of people who had it way worse than he did. People with no homes, people with no jobs, people with no food. But in those moments where you feel in despair, it's hard to compare your situation to anyone else's. He tried to be grateful for what he did have—a place to rest his head, good friends, and reasonably decent health if you took the shoulder out of the equation. But he felt blocked. He didn't have empathy for other people like he knew he should. He could only think of himself, and that fact alone made him angry.

He was so lost in his thoughts that he almost missed seeing her. Luna was sitting on a yoga mat near the water's edge. She was obviously meditating because her eyes were closed. It was something he never understood himself, but she had the most peaceful look on her face. There had never been a time in his life when his mind felt that quiet.

The rising sun caught the loose strands of her long black hair, and despite himself, he found his steps toward her slowing. She was a beautiful woman—petite, with bronzed skin and that beautiful head of hair. He couldn't remember seeing a more beautiful head of hair in his life, to be honest.

He thought about their brief encounter at the café and winced. He'd been unnecessarily harsh about her work, letting his own bitterness spill out onto somebody who was just trying to help people, including him. He knew how it felt to have people criticize what you did for a living, but even worse was when it was your passion. Dawson's words from the front porch the other night echoed in his mind.

Luna's eyes suddenly opened, and she caught him staring at her. For a moment, they just looked at each other across the sand with the sound of the waves crashing, filling the silence between them.

"Well, good morning," she called out.

Archer pretended he hadn't heard her and continued his walk. It would be easier than facing the awkwardness he had created in their last interaction.

Something, maybe Dawson's voice rolling around in his head, or maybe just plain guilt, made him stop in his tracks.

"Morning," he replied, taking a few steps closer. "You're up bright and early."

"Well, I like to start my day early here," she said, uncrossing her legs and stretching them in front of her. "I find that the ocean has a way of clearing your mind."

His hands shifted uncomfortably, finding their

way into his back pockets. "Yeah, I suppose that's why I'm out here, too."

She studied him for a moment, and he fought the urge to look away from her gaze.

"How's your shoulder?" she asked.

The question caught him off guard. Most people in town tiptoed around the subject of his injury, acting like it was some kind of taboo topic no one was supposed to bring up.

"It's fine," he said automatically. "Well, I guess as fine as it can be."

"You favor it when you walk," she observed. "Have you tried any gentle stretching or movement therapy?"

He felt his defenses rising up like a wall around a castle. "Look, I've got physical therapists for that. I don't need—"

"I'm not trying to fix you, Archer," Luna interrupted, holding up her hand. "I was just making an observation."

The wind picked up, carrying the scent of salt and seaweed. Archer watched as Luna gathered her long hair and put it in a knot at the nape of her neck. The simple gesture seemed to diffuse some of the tension hanging in the air.

"I'm sorry," he said finally. "I mean about what I said at the café. Your work being, you know…"

"Oh, you mean about my life's work being 'woo-

woo stuff'?" Luna's lips curved into a small smile, and he hated to admit that it gave him some butterflies in his stomach. It wasn't really a very manly thing to say out loud.

"Yeah, that. I was having a bad day."

"Seems like you have a lot of those lately," she said. There was no judgment in her tone.

He let out a humorless laugh. "I guess you could say that."

She stood up and brushed the sand from her yoga pants. "You know, sometimes the hardest part isn't the physical pain. Often it's the stories we tell ourselves about who we are without that thing we lost. I've dealt with that with a lot of clients."

"You sound like a therapist."

"Hmm, funny how that works," she said with a hint of amusement. "Well, I should get going. Janine's coming by to plan out our first yoga sessions."

She rolled up her mat and tucked it under her arm. "You're welcome to join us anytime, you know. No pressure or expectations. Just breathing and moving at your own pace."

"I'll think about it," he said, although he knew they probably both realized he wouldn't.

She nodded and started walking back toward Serenity. She paused after a few steps and turned back. "You know, Archer, sometimes the bravest thing we can do is admit that we need help, even if it's just learning how to breathe again."

He watched her walk away, her words settling into the spaces between his thoughts. The sun had fully risen, painting the beach in shades of gold. Archer stood there for a long time, just listening to the waves and wondering when breathing had become so complicated.

L una's hands trembled slightly as she unlocked her front door. Her encounter with Archer on the beach had left her feeling a bit unsettled, although not necessarily in a bad way. There had been something in his eyes when she talked about breathing, a flash of vulnerability that he had quickly attempted to hide. Or maybe she was just having low blood sugar and needed to eat an orange.

"Well, you're back early," Janine's cheerful voice broke through her thoughts. She was already on the yoga deck, setting up for their morning session together. They had decided to do a couple of sessions just to make sure that it was everything Luna wanted for her clients.

"Oh, you know, I was doing my morning meditation on the beach," Luna said, dropping her mat by the door, "and then I ran into Archer Hawk."

Janine's eyebrows shot up. "Really? And how did that go?"

"Well, I guess better than our first meeting," Luna said as she started arranging some meditation cushions. "He actually did apologize for being rude at the café."

"Archer Hawk apologized?" Janine let out a low whistle. "That's unexpected. I've heard he's not exactly known for admitting when he's wrong."

Luna thought about his stiff posture and the way he'd struggled to meet her eyes. "He's hurting, and not just physically."

"Well, I guess you'd be hurting if you'd lost everything you'd worked for," SuAnn's voice boomed from the doorway. She stood there holding a box from Hotcakes. "Lord knows that boy never has seemed to handle his feelings properly, from what I've heard."

"Mama!" Janine said with a hint of warning in her voice. "What brings you by?"

"Well, can't a mother bring breakfast to her daughter?" SuAnn set the box down nearby. "Besides, I wanted to see how things were coming along here. You know, the whole town's talking about your opening next week, Luna."

"Good things, I hope," Luna said, her stomach fluttering with nerves.

"I think it's mostly curiosity," SuAnn said, opening the box and revealing an assortment of muffins. It looked like everything from chocolate to blueberry. "Though some folks wonder if Seagrove needs all this alternative healing business."

"Mama!" Janine said again, more firmly this time.

Luna just smiled. "It's okay. It's not really alternative healing because I am a therapist, and these are proven modalities, but I know what I'm offering isn't for everybody. For the people who need it, I hope Serenity can be a safe place to heal."

SuAnn's expression softened. "Well, when you put it that way..." She pulled out a muffin and handed it to Luna. "Here, try this. This is a new recipe, lavender lemon. I thought it might fit with your whole wellness theme."

Luna took a bite. "This is amazing!"

"Of course it is," SuAnn said with a satisfied smile. "Now, about that opening celebration."

"Opening celebration?" Luna asked, taking another bite.

"Well, you can't just open your doors quietly and expect people to wander in." SuAnn settled into one of the deck chairs. "This is Seagrove. We celebrate everything, and a new business, especially one like this, well, it deserves a proper welcome."

Janine rolled her eyes affectionately. "Here we go. Mama's in party-planning mode."

"I was just thinking something simple," Luna began, but SuAnn waved her hand dismissively.

"Simple doesn't get people talking, honey. Now, I've already spoken to Julie about setting up a book display from Down Yonder—you know, wellness books, meditation guides, that sort of thing. I think Dixie's on board, too. Naturally, I'll handle the refreshments."

Luna glanced at Janine, who shrugged with a smile that seemed to say, *just go with it.*

"I appreciate the thought, SuAnn, but I don't want anything too elaborate. The whole point of Serenity is peace and calm. It's not really a party atmosphere."

"Oh, we can do peaceful," SuAnn assured her, "but peaceful doesn't have to mean boring. I mean, what if we did like a sunset gathering? String up more of those little lights over on the pergola, serve some healthy appetizers. I've been experimenting with some gluten-free recipes that would be perfect. Janine could lead a yoga demonstration."

Despite her initial resistance, Luna found herself warming up to the idea. "You know, that actually sounds kind of nice."

"Of course it does," SuAnn said, looking pleased. "It'll give people the chance to see what you're about. Some people just need to experience things for themselves before they can understand it."

Luna thought about Archer on the beach and how he seemed almost interested despite himself. "That is true."

"Speaking of which," SuAnn continued, "I heard you had a run-in with our resident grumpy golf pro this morning."

Luna looked over at Janine, who held up her hands. "Don't look at me, I just found out. News travels fast around here."

"It wasn't a run-in," Luna said. "We just happened to be on the beach at the same time."

SuAnn hummed, clearly not buying the casual dismissal. "Well, make sure you send him an invitation to the opening, because that boy needs what you're offering here, whether he knows that or not."

"Mama..." Janine warned again.

"What? I'm just saying what everyone's thinking." SuAnn stood and smoothed out her skirt. "Now I need to get back to the bakery. I'll start working on the menu for the opening. But Luna, honey, don't you worry about a thing. We'll make sure Serenity gets the proper welcome it deserves."

After SuAnn left, Janine turned to her with an apologetic smile. "Sorry about that. Once my mama gets an idea in her head—"

"It's okay," Luna said. "Actually, it's kind of nice. Back in Austin, I just felt so alone. Here, it's like I suddenly have this whole new family full of people supporting me."

"Well, that's Seagrove for you," Janine said, rolling out her yoga mat. "We might be in each other's business just a little too much sometimes, but when it counts, we're there for each other."

Luna looked out over the ocean, thinking about the upcoming opening, about SuAnn's determination to make everything special, and about Archer's guarded vulnerability. Maybe this was what she needed—not just for Serenity, but for herself too.

"Now," Janine said, "let's plan this yoga demonstration, because if I know my mama, half the town's going to be here. We want to show them just how magical this place can be."

Luna nodded, reaching for her own mat. They started working through the poses, the ocean breeze carrying the scent of salt and possibility.

CHAPTER 4

Archer stood in front of the mirror at the inn and adjusted the collar of his button-down pale pink shirt. The invitation to Serenity's opening celebration sat on the dresser, its elegant script glaring at him from a few feet away. Julie had hand-delivered it yesterday, giving him a look that showed no argument was necessary about his attendance.

"Well, you clean up nice," Dawson said from the doorway. "Although you might want to do something about that scowl. It's a party, not a funeral."

"Remind me again why I have to go to this thing?" Archer grumbled, running a hand through his hair.

"Because my wife asked you to. And when she asks you to do something, you just do it. It's also the polite thing to do. And maybe, just maybe, it won't kill you to be a part of this community again. You did grow up here, after all."

Archer turned to face him. "I saw Luna on the beach the other morning."

"Oh?" Dawson's expression remained carefully neutral, but Archer could definitely see the interest in his eyes.

"She was different, I guess, than I expected." Archer picked up the invitation and ran his thumb over the embossed lettering. "She didn't try to push anything on me. We just talked about breathing, of all things."

"Imagine that," Dawson said dryly. "A therapist and wellness expert talking about breathing? That's revolutionary stuff."

"You're real funny," Archer said. "I just don't know what I'm supposed to do at this thing."

Dawson put his hands on Archer's shoulders. "You show up, be pleasant, eat some of SuAnn's food. It's really not that complicated, man."

It sure felt complicated. Everything he did felt complicated these days.

"Look," Dawson said, leaning against the door-frame. "I know this isn't easy for you. Being back here, seeing everybody, watching them walk on eggshells around you, which I'm not going to do, by the way."

"They don't all walk on eggshells," Archer

muttered, thinking of Dixie's direct stares and SuAnn's not-so-subtle comments whenever he stopped by Hotcakes.

"True, but some of them just hit you over the head with their concern, and they mean well. This is a celebration for Luna and the community. It's about welcoming someone new, someone who might actually be good for this town."

Archer thought about Luna at the beach and the quiet strength in her voice when she talked about breathing. There had been no judgment there, no pressure. She was just making an observation, but it was still an invitation he wasn't ready to accept.

"Julie says she's different," Archer said, adjusting his cuffs. "Says she's not just another outsider trying to come in and change Seagrove."

"And what do you think about that?"

Archer met Dawson's eyes in the mirror. "I think maybe she understands more than I gave her credit for at first."

A knowing smile spread across Dawson's face. "Well, would you look at that? The mighty Archer Hawk admitting he might have been wrong about something."

"Don't push it," Archer warned. "Let's just get this over with."

As they headed downstairs, Julie was waiting in

the foyer, looking elegant in a flowy sundress. She gave Archer an approving nod.

"You look nice. Very ungrumpy."

"Thanks, I think," Archer said.

The sun was starting to set as they made their way toward Serenity, painting the sky in shades of pink and gold. Archer could see the glow of fairy lights in the distance strung along the yoga deck and hear the soft murmur of voices carried by the ocean breeze. He took a deep breath, remembering Luna's words about breathing being the bravest thing sometimes. It made him feel a little better.

Maybe she had a point after all.

Luna stood on Serenity's front porch, looking at the transformation SuAnn and the others had created. Fairy lights twinkled overhead, casting a warm glow over the gathering crowd. The ocean breeze carried a mingling of scents—from the appetizers SuAnn had insisted on preparing to the salty air that hung there naturally. There was a mix of healthy food and irresistible comfort food that somehow managed to please everyone.

"Well, this is just gorgeous," Julie said, walking up to her with a glass of sparkling water with a strawberry floating in it. "You've created something really special here, Luna."

"Well, I had a lot of help," she said, smiling as she watched Dixie talking to a group of people near the yoga deck. It appeared to be a very animated story.

"Still, it takes a lot of vision to see what this place could be," Julie said. "I mean, look how many people came."

"I don't think I expected such a big turnout." Luna nodded, her throat tight with emotion. The turnout was even better than she had ever hoped for. She was sure some people were skeptical and just curious about this new addition to the community. It was her job to educate them and make them realize that she could be of help in their lives.

Her eyes caught movement at the edge of the crowd, and then her breath hitched slightly when she saw Archer standing off to the side with Dawson. He looked very handsome in his crisp button-down shirt and dark jeans. He looked less guarded somehow.

"He cleans up pretty nice, doesn't he?" Julie said with a knowing smile.

"I didn't expect him to come," Luna admitted.

"Well, Archer surprises people sometimes, though usually not in good ways lately."

Luna laughed, but before she could respond, she

spotted her first official client arriving. She moved over to greet the woman and noticed Archer watching her from across the deck. Their eyes met briefly, and she offered a small smile before turning to her client. It was a woman in town who had signed up for some therapy sessions after a particularly devastating loss in her life.

As the evening flowed smoothly, Janine led a short sunset yoga demonstration that even seemed to intrigue some skeptics. Of course, Janine taught yoga classes at her own studio, and Luna would never want to do anything to take away from that, but Janine had pointed out that many people would probably sign up for classes here because it was overlooking the ocean, and she was happy to do it.

Luna moved through the crowd, answering questions about her programs and services and sharing her vision for what Serenity could be. Later, she found herself alone on the open deck, just taking a moment to breathe and center herself. The party-goers had moved inside, taking tours of the place and eating some of SuAnn's new lavender lemon cupcakes .

"Nice turnout," a familiar deep voice said from behind her.

She turned around to find Archer standing there, his hands in his pockets, looking slightly uncom-fortable.

"Thank you for coming," she said softly. "It means

a lot to have the community's support. Even from the resident skeptic."

His lips moved in a way that might have been the beginning of a smile, but it quickly dropped back down. "You like having comments from skeptics?"

"Especially from the skeptics. They keep me honest."

Archer moved to stand beside her at the railing, both of them looking out at the darkening ocean.

"You know, I've been wondering about something," he said after a moment.

"Just one thing?" she asked.

He looked over at her, and in the soft glow of the fairy lights, she could see the ghost of a smile on his lips.

"One thing for now. Why Seagrove, out of all the places you could have chosen?"

Luna smiled. "Would you believe I only came here once when I was a little kid? My parents saved for years to take that vacation."

"Just once? And it made that much of an impression?"

She nodded. "Some places just speak to your soul, you know. My *abuela*, my grandmother on my mother's side, used to say that about Puerto Rico. I spent summers with her there when I was young. It was the most beautiful place. The beaches, the culture, the food—everything was alive with color and music."

"So why not open Serenity there instead?" he asked.

She was quiet for a moment. "Puerto Rico was my mother's home, her history. But Seagrove—it was the first place I chose for myself. It was one childhood vacation to everybody else. And it wasn't about heritage or family obligations. It was just peace to me. Pure, simple peace. The kind that settles into your bones and never leaves."

She could feel Archer studying her. "You remembered Seagrove that clearly?"

"Oh, I remember everything. Making sandcastles that the tide would take away. Looking for shells in the morning mist. Watching the sunset paint the sky in colors I'd never seen before. The smell of the marsh, the sound of the birds. My parents couldn't afford a fancy hotel or any of the touristy stuff, but it didn't matter. Seagrove was magic all by itself."

The breeze picked up, carrying the sound of laughter from inside. Luna wrapped her arms around herself.

"I get that," he said, his voice quieter. "The magic part. Before everything happened, there was nothing better than being on the course at dawn when the dew was still fresh on the grass and everything was quiet except for the birds."

Luna turned to him, a bit surprised by the vulnerability in his voice. "You miss it."

It wasn't a question, but he answered anyway. "Every day, every minute."

"Well, sometimes the things we miss the most are just the feelings they gave us, not the things themselves."

His jaw tightened. "You sound like a therapist again."

"Funny how that keeps happening," she said with a small smile. "Must be because I *am* one."

Before he could respond, SuAnn's voice rolled outside. "Luna, honey, you've got to come try these empanadas I made! I had to call my friend three times to get the recipe right."

Luna laughed and shook her head. "That woman is unstoppable."

"Julie would say you have no idea," Archer said. "Better not keep her waiting. I think she's known to track people down."

As Luna turned to go inside, she paused. "I'm glad you came tonight, Archer. I hope you are, too."

She left him there on the deck and could feel his eyes following her. She wondered if maybe, just maybe, they had taken a small step toward understanding each other.

❧

The morning after the opening celebration, Archer was back on the beach for his usual walk at dawn. His mind kept going back to the conversation he had with Luna on the yoga deck. There was something about the way she talked about Seagrove, about how she found peace there, that had struck a chord with him. He'd grown up in Seagrove, so he knew every inch of it like the back of his hand, even after not living there for so many years. And he wondered if now, as an adult, he could recapture the experience that he'd had as a child. The mysteriousness of the Lowcountry—the smells, the sights, the sounds. Could he appreciate them and allow them to find peace for him, that elusive thing that he seemed to be unable to find?

He flexed his shoulder absentmindedly, feeling that familiar ache that always seemed worse in the morning humidity. The physical therapist had, of course, given him tons of exercises to do, but most days he couldn't even bring himself to complete them. What was the point? His career was over, and there was no amount of stretching or strengthening that was going to change that. He felt like such a feeble old man, but Luna's words kept echoing in his head.

Sometimes the things we miss most are the feelings they gave us, not the things themselves.

"Dang therapist," he muttered, kicking at the sand.

"Do you talk to yourself often?"

Archer turned to see Dawson jogging up behind him, already sweaty from his morning run.

"Just thinking out loud because I thought I was alone, but apparently I have a weirdo stalker," Archer said.

"Thinking about last night?" Dawson fell into step beside him. "Saw you talking with Luna."

"Oh gosh, don't start," Archer warned. "It's way too early in the morning for this."

"Start what? I'm just making an observation," Dawson grinned. "Although I have to say, it's the most I've seen you talk to anybody since you got back."

Archer was quiet for a moment, watching a flock of seabirds overhead. "Well, she's a little different than I expected."

"Different good or different bad?"

"Just different," Archer shrugged and winced as his shoulder protested. "It's like she gets it somehow, about places and things having magic, and about finding peace in unexpected ways or in certain places."

"You mean like on a golf course at dawn?"

"Yeah," Archer said. "Like that."

They walked in silence for a while, the waves providing a steady rhythm to their steps.

"You know," Dawson said after a while, "Julie told me that Luna's going to start some gentle movement classes this week. Not exactly yoga, but something about breathing and mindful stretching."

Archer shot him a look. "Are you seriously suggesting—"

"I'm not suggesting anything," Dawson interrupted, holding up his hands. "I'm just sharing information. I like to spread the news. But since you brought it up, it might not be the worst idea for you. It's better than walking around with your shoulder locked up like it's in a vice. I swear it looks like it's stuck to your ear nowadays."

They passed Serenity, with its pale pink exterior glowing in the early morning light. Through the large windows, Archer could barely see Luna moving around inside, setting up for the day. He felt a strong pull there for some reason, like he wanted to go up there and have a cup of coffee or just sit and watch her move around. Maybe he was becoming a stalker.

She paused at one of the windows, looking out at the ocean, and for a moment he could see what she meant about finding peace here. He could see it right on her face.

"You know she talked about Puerto Rico last

night," Archer said. "About how she could have opened her center there, but she chose here instead because of one vacation when she was a kid."

"Sometimes that's all it takes," Dawson said. "One moment, one place, one feeling that changes everything. Just like when I met Julie. Just like the first time you picked up a golf club."

That memory hit Archer hard. He could feel the weight of his father's old club in his hands and the perfect arc of his first real drive. The feeling that he had finally found his thing that made this world make sense.

"That's not fair," he muttered.

"What's not fair? Reminding you that you used to love something purely for how it made you feel and not for all those trophies or rankings or titles?"

Archer stopped walking and turned to face him. "What's your point, Dawson?"

"My point is that it's time to find that feeling again, just like Luna said. Maybe that feeling's not going to be in golf but in something else. And maybe," Dawson glanced back at Serenity, "maybe someone who understands about magic and peace would be able to help you with that."

Before Archer could respond, Dawson's phone buzzed. He checked it and grimaced. "Julie needs me back at the inn. Think about what I said, okay? And maybe try moving that shoulder a bit before it freezes completely."

As Dawson jogged away, Archer stood there at the water's edge, watching the waves roll in. Through the windows of Serenity, he could still see Luna moving around, preparing for whatever her first big day might bring. The morning sun caught her dark hair as she worked, and something in his chest tightened.

Maybe Dawson had a point.

Maybe it was time to try something different.

Maybe.

He shook his head and turned back toward the inn, one step at a time. For now, he was going to finish his morning walk, and his thoughts would have to wait. But he couldn't help glancing back one more time at the pale pink building that actually seemed to hold some possibilities.

CHAPTER 5

Luna walked around Serenity's main room, lighting lavender-scented candles and adjusting meditation cushions. Today was her first official morning session. Through the windows, she had seen Archer and Dawson walking on the beach earlier, but she pretended that she was just working and not paying any attention to them. She did notice they were having quite an intense conversation and that caught her attention.

A knock at the door pulled her from her thoughts. Janine stood there with her yoga mat tucked under her arm.

"Ready for our first real day?" Janine asked as she stepped inside.

"As ready as I'll ever be," Luna replied. She smoothed her hands over her bright pink yoga pants. "I keep thinking I've forgotten something important."

"Like breathing?" Janine teased as she set her mat on the deck. Luna liked to keep the French doors open so that the house was open to the ocean. It was one of her favorite things about facing the beach—to feel that ocean breeze coming right through the room.

"Maybe that's it. I should probably breathe," Luna laughed.

"I saw Archer out walking this morning," Janine said casually—a little too casually. "He seemed very interested in what you were doing in here."

"Yes, I saw him and Dawson. He's just curious," Luna said, arranging some fresh flowers in a vase. "And probably wondering what kind of a crazy person opens this kind of a place in his tiny hometown."

"Mm-hmm." Janine's tone was skeptical. "Well, my mama thinks—"

"If you finish that sentence with anything about me and Archer Hawk dating or getting married or having babies, I'm going to revoke your yoga privileges," Luna warned.

Janine laughed and stretched out her mat. "All I'm saying is he actually came to the opening celebration, and from what Julie told me, he stayed longer than they expected."

"Look, I would only want to help him in a professional manner. He obviously has lots of issues, and I feel sorry for him. I feel empathy for him as another human being. But can we just focus on today?" Luna asked, even though she was trying not to smile as she thought about him despite herself. "Our first real clients will be here in less than an hour."

"Okay, fine, change the subject," Janine said. "But you can't blame me for being interested. Apparently, Archer hasn't shown interest in anything or anyone since he came back to Seagrove."

Luna arranged teacups on a tray. She brought special herbs from her stash, planning to brew her grandmother's calming tea blend for after the morning session.

"And you know what I think?" Janine continued, sitting on her mat. "I think you understand him better than most people here. We all just see the golf guy who lost his career, but you see—"

"I see a person underneath their pain," Luna finished quietly. "It's not that complicated, Janine. It's what I'm trained to do. It doesn't mean I'm interested in him at all beyond that."

"Are you sure that's all it is? Professional interest?"

Before Luna could respond, the front door opened, and their clients started to arrive—a mother and daughter from Atlanta who'd booked a week-long vacation to Seagrove and wanted some day sessions at Serenity. Luna straightened her shoulders and pushed thoughts of Archer aside. Time to get to work, she whispered to Janine, standing up to greet her guests.

As she led them through Serenity's morning routine of gentle stretching, meditation, and finally the special tea, Luna couldn't completely shake the memory of Archer on the beach that morning, looking up at her windows.

As Luna poured the herbal tea into delicate cups with little pink roses on them, she watched her clients' faces soften with contentment. Their morning session had gone better than she'd hoped. Even the teenage daughter who had started the class with typical adolescent skepticism gradually relaxed into the gentle movements and breathing exercises.

"Wow, this tea is amazing," her mother, Sarah, said after taking a sip. "I've never tasted anything quite like this."

"It's my grandmother's blend," Luna explained, sitting down on one of the cushions across from them. "She grew all these herbs in her garden in Puerto Rico. She always said that a good tea was medicine for the soul."

"Well, your grandmother sounds very wise," Sarah said, cradling her cup in both hands.

"She was," Luna said, remembering her abuela's

small but vibrant garden. "She taught me that healing isn't about just fixing what's wrong, but about nurturing what's right."

The door opened, and Luna looked up to see Julie entering with a stack of books from Down Yonder Bookstore.

"I'm so sorry to interrupt," Julie said. "I didn't know you had clients here this morning, but I brought those wellness books we discussed for your lending library."

"Oh, perfect timing," Luna said. "We were just finishing up our morning session."

Julie set the books on the shelves, and Sarah and her daughter gathered their things. Both looked noticeably more relaxed than when they had arrived. Luna walked them to the door and scheduled their next session for the following morning.

"You're good at this," Julie said once they were alone. "Really good. They looked like the two most relaxed people on the planet."

Luna smiled. "Well, that's the goal. Small changes, one breath at a time."

Julie walked over to the window and looked out at the ocean. "I'll never get tired of this view, no matter if I see it here or at my own house. You know, I was thinking about those gentle movement classes you mentioned starting, the ones for people with injuries or chronic pain."

Luna smiled, already knowing where this was heading. "Let me guess, you think they'd be perfect for a certain former golfer?"

"Well, now that you mention it," Julie turned to face her. "He's not doing his physical therapy exercises. Dawson's very worried about him. My husband is the sweetest man. He always thinks about other people more than himself, but honestly, I'm worried about him, too."

Luna began gathering up the empty teacups. "Julie, I understand you want to help him, but Archer needs to want help first. I can't force him to come here. He needs to do it for the right reasons."

"You know, he's very different with you," Julie said. "At the opening celebration, he was actually talking to you. Apparently, he really talked, not just grunted one-word responses like he usually does."

"We just connected over something unexpected," Luna said. "That's all."

"Well, maybe that's enough. Sometimes all it takes is just that one small connection to open a door."

Luna carried the teacups to the kitchen, thinking about Archer's face when he talked about missing the golf course in the mornings. There was something there—such a longing, such grief for something lost.

"I'll tell you what," Luna said. "If he asks about the classes, and that's a big if, I'll make sure that there's space for him. But it has to be his choice, Julie. You can't heal someone who's not ready."

Julie nodded. "Fair enough. Though don't be surprised if Mama starts leaving class schedules at his table every time he comes into Hotcakes."

Luna laughed. "Is there anything SuAnn won't do to get her way?"

"Not that I've discovered yet," Julie said with a grin. "Oh, speaking of Mama, she wanted me to remind you about Sunday dinner, and no excuses this time. She said you need to experience a proper Seagrove family meal."

Luna wiped her hands on a tea towel, trying to hide her nervousness. "Sunday dinner? Listen, I don't want to impose on a family gathering."

"Impose?" Julie laughed. "Luna, you clearly don't understand how things work here. Family isn't just about blood in Seagrove. Besides, Mama's already planned the menu. She's determined to try her hand at more Puerto Rican dishes, so we're going to need the backup."

"Oh no," Luna said. "Please tell me she's not going to attempt mofongo."

"Actually, I think that was exactly what she was muttering about this morning. Something about plantains and garlic."

"That's it. I have to come now, if only to prevent a

culinary disaster." Luna shook her head. "Your mother is a force of nature."

"Well, that she is," Julie said. "Speaking of forces of nature, Dixie's coming, too. She needs to properly educate you about Seagrove's history, she says."

Luna loved Dixie and her energy. "Well, I have a feeling I'm in for quite an education, then."

"Oh, you have no idea," Julie said. "But that's what makes it home. You know, you're going to fit in here just fine."

Home. It was starting to feel that way, wasn't it? Luna thought.

The door opened again, and both women turned to see who had arrived. Luna was shocked, and her breath caught in her throat when she saw Archer standing in the doorway, looking uncomfortable.

"Well, I'll let you get back to work," Julie said, quickly gathering her things. As she passed Archer, she gave him a surprised smile. "Well, look who finally decided to stop lurking outside."

Luna watched Julie and Janine leave and then turned to Archer, who stood just inside the doorway as if he was going to run out at any moment. He looked like he wasn't even sure how he'd gotten there.

"Good morning," she said, trying to sound casual. "Can I offer you some tea?"

He shifted his weight, his hand unconsciously

moving to his shoulder. "I, um, actually came here to ask about those movement classes you're starting next week. Julie mentioned them."

Of course she did, Luna thought, making a mental note to have a word with her new friend about meddling. "Would you like to sit down? I can tell you about them."

Archer hesitated and then nodded, following her to the comfortable seating area overlooking the ocean. Luna noticed how carefully he lowered himself into the chair.

"So the classes are designed for people working through chronic pain and injuries," she explained. "It's about gentle movement, breathing techniques that help release tension and promote healing."

"So no weird music or chanting?" he asked.

She couldn't tell, but there seemed to be a hint of humor in his voice.

Luna smiled. "No chanting. That's a different class," she said, laughing. "Though I can't guarantee there won't be some calming background music, but the ocean does a lot of the work for us there."

She watched as his eyes drifted to the windows.

"I'm not good at this stuff," he finally said, looking back at her. "The slow movement, the breathing. I'm used to pushing through pain, not doing... well, whatever this is that you do."

"And how's that working out for you?" Luna asked gently.

His eyes met hers. "Not great," he admitted.

Luna leaned forward slightly, keeping her voice gentle. "Can I ask you something, Archer?"

He nodded, but she could see wariness creep into his face.

"What do you miss most about golf? Not the competition or the rankings, but the feeling of it."

He was so quiet for so long that she thought he might not answer at all. Finally, he spoke. "The peace. Early morning on the course, when everything's quiet except for the birds and the sound of my club cutting through the air. The whoosh of that sound, the perfect connection between me and the club and the ball, when everything aligns just right. The way nothing else existed in those moments."

"And that's what these classes are about," Luna said softly. "Finding that peace again, that perfect alignment, but just in a different way."

Archer ran his hand through his hair. "I saw you working with those clients this morning," he said, "when I was walking for my second time. They looked content, peaceful."

"That's the goal. Small changes, one breath at a time."

"You said that before on the beach—about breathing."

"Because it's true."

She stood and moved to the small kitchen area. "Let me make you some tea, my grandmother's blend. No pressure about the classes, just tea."

She could feel him watching her as she prepared the tea, and when she returned with two cups, he had relaxed a little.

"Your grandmother," he said, as she handed him the cup. "The one from Puerto Rico?"

Luna nodded and sat back in her chair. "She would have loved this place. She always said the ocean was its own special medicine."

Archer took a careful sip, his eyebrows raising slightly. "This is different, but good different."

"It's a blend of herbs my *abuela* grew herself. Mint for clarity, chamomile for calm, and a few other special ingredients she swore by. She used to say that the best medicine doesn't come from a doctor's office."

"Smart woman," Archer said. "The movement classes—when do they start?"

Luna kept her voice steady. "Tuesday and Thursday mornings, right after sunrise. Small groups, just four or five people. And no pressure to commit to anything. You can try one class and see how it feels."

He nodded, tapping his fingers against the teacup. "Maybe... maybe I'll try one."

"I'll save you a spot," Luna said, trying not to show how she was cheering inside of her head. "Just remember, it's not about pushing through pain. It's about working with your body, not against it."

"Yeah, that's the hard part," he admitted. "I've spent my whole life pushing. I don't know how to do it any other way."

"Well, maybe it's time to learn," Luna said. "Sometimes the bravest thing we can do is just try something new."

"I should go," Archer said, setting down his empty cup. "Thanks for the tea. And the, well, you know…"

"Lack of pressure?" Luna suggested.

"Yeah, that."

He stood carefully and walked toward the door. "I'll see you Tuesday, I guess."

"Tuesday," she confirmed. "Just bring yourself and an open mind. That's all you're going to need."

As she watched him walk away, she felt a mixture of hope and anxiety. This was either the beginning of something important or a recipe for heartache. But as her *abuela* used to say, the best things in life usually came with a little risk.

Archer sat in his room at the inn, staring at the workout clothes he'd put out for tomorrow's class. What in the world was he thinking, agreeing to this? He could already hear the whispers that would probably spread around town—how the fallen professional golfer was reduced to a gentle movement class at some kind of new-age woo-woo wellness center.

A knock at the door interrupted his brooding.

"It's open," he called, knowing it would be Dawson. Who else would it be?

His friend stepped in and looked at the workout clothes and Archer's troubled facial expression. "So you must have gone to see her."

"Julie told you?"

"Nah, she didn't have to. You've just got that look like you used to get before a big tournament, like you're simultaneously plotting to win and planning your escape route."

Archer laughed. "It's just a movement class, man. It's not the Masters."

"Right." Dawson leaned against the dresser. "And that's why you're sitting here staring at workout clothes like they might bite you."

"I don't know why I agreed to this," Archer said under his breath.

"Yeah, you do. You agreed because, for the first

time since you got injured, somebody is offering to help you without making you feel like a broken man."

"What's that supposed to mean?" Archer asked, looking up sharply.

"It means Luna sees you as a person. She refuses to see you as a tragedy, which is what you see when you think of yourself. Maybe that scares you more than any amount of physical pain."

Archer stood up and walked to the window. "You're starting to sound just like her, you know. All this talk of feelings and seeing people for who they are."

"Well, maybe that's because she's right," Dawson said. "When was the last time you did something just because it might help, not because you were trying to prove something or be the best?"

The question hit harder than Archer wanted to admit. His whole life had been about proving things —proving he was good enough, proving he deserved his spot on the tour, proving he would come back from every single setback, no matter how big it was. Until this one. This one had taken him out. If not physically forever, then definitely mentally. He knew his professional career was over.

"Her tea was different," he suddenly said, surprising himself.

"Her what?"

"Her tea. She gave me some blend that her grand-mother in Puerto Rico made. It was..." He struggled to find the right words. "It was like nothing I've ever tasted before. Then she talked about her grand-mother and about finding peace in certain places. I don't know, it all made sense at the time somehow."

Dawson was quiet for a moment. "You know what I think?"

"I'm one-hundred percent sure you're going to tell me."

"I think you've spent so long being Archer Hawk, the golf pro, that you've forgotten how to just be Archer. And maybe that's what really scares you about going to these classes. It's not the breathing or the movement or any of that stuff. It's the fact that, for an hour, you'll just have to be yourself."

Archer turned to him. "When did you become so philosophical?"

"Probably around the time I married a bookstore owner," Dawson said, laughing. "I guess Julie's rubbing off on me."

"God help us all," Archer muttered.

"Well, either way, I stand by what I said. I remember the guy you were when we were growing up. And this isn't him."

"Well, there's a lot of water under the bridge as we get older," Archer said, shrugging.

"I know you're still in there. And I liked that guy."

"Are you saying you don't like *this* guy?"

"He's okay," Dawson said, smiling. "But I know he can be better. You need to get back to who you were as a person, without all the other stuff. I think that's the only way you're ever going to be happy."

"Well, the problem is, I have no idea how to do that."

"Speaking of Julie," Dawson said, changing the subject, "she mentioned SuAnn invited you to Sunday dinner?"

Archer groaned. "Does everybody in town know my business?"

"Pretty much. Small town. You remember that. Besides, SuAnn's Sunday dinners are legendary around here. And she's apparently going to try her hand at Puerto Rican cuisine."

"Ah, so let me guess. Luna's going to be there."

Dawson's grin widened. "Now why would that matter?"

"It absolutely doesn't matter," Archer said a little too quickly. "I just don't need the whole town watching me like I'm some kind of project they need to fix."

"Nobody's trying to fix you, man. They're trying to include you. There's a difference. Stop being so defensive."

Archer looked back at the workout clothes on the bed. He'd laid out a simple gray T-shirt and black shorts, but today they were mocking him. How many times had he gotten dressed for practice without a second thought? And now, all of a sudden, this felt very complicated.

"You know what Luna said? She said sometimes the bravest thing we can do is try something new."

"Smart woman," Dawson said.

"Yeah. Yeah, I think she is."

The sound of the ocean drifted through the open window. It was steady and constant. It never stopped. It came in, it went out—much like breathing, he thought. And then he remembered Luna's words about working with his body instead of against it.

"So," Dawson said, "I'll tell Julie you'll be at Sunday dinner?"

Archer sighed. "Do I really have a choice?"

"In this town, with these particular women?" Dawson laughed. "Not really."

After Dawson left, Archer found himself drawn to the window again. From his room at the inn, he could see Serenity's pale pink exterior off in the distance. A light was still on inside, and he could make out Luna's silhouette moving around, probably preparing for tomorrow's classes. He thought about the tea she'd given him, how the unfamiliar blend of herbs had somehow calmed the constant tension in his shoulder, how she'd talked about her grandmother's garden in Puerto Rico but had chosen Seagrove instead.

He got that—how a place could call to you, how it could feel like home even when it didn't make any sense on paper. That's how the golf course had always felt to him. It didn't matter which golf course he was on, they all felt like home. When he didn't look down and see bright green grass, perfectly manicured, it felt weird to him.

His phone buzzed on the nightstand—another message from his agent that he ignored. What could he say? *Sorry, can't think about comebacks right now. I'm too busy drinking herbal tea and signing up for gentle movement classes.*

But Luna's voice echoed in his head. *Sometimes the things we miss the most are the feelings they gave us, not the things themselves.*

He looked at his workout clothes again. They were simple and basic, unlike the high-tech gear he'd worn on tour. But maybe that was the point. Maybe Dawson was right. It was time to strip everything back to the basics, including himself.

The only problem was, he didn't remember that guy or what he was like.

One breath at a time, he muttered to himself.

CHAPTER 6

L una woke before dawn and walked into the living room to start moving through her morning routine. Routine was a big part of her life. She had quite a dysfunctional childhood at different moments, and having a routine had kept her sane over the years. She brewed a fresh batch of her abuela's tea blend and stepped out onto the deck to watch the sky lighten over the ocean. She couldn't imagine a time where this would ever get old. She had dreamed of being in Seagrove her entire life, and now she finally lived here and could look at this view every day. She wondered if other people got used to it after a while, but she vowed to herself it would never become just a humdrum part of her day. She would appreciate it with as much gratitude as she could muster.

Today was important. This was the first gentle movement class she would teach in Seagrove, and she knew Archer would be among the students. She'd spent extra time planning the session because she wanted to strike the perfect balance between accessible and therapeutic. After finishing the tea, she moved to the main space, lighting candles and opening windows. There was nothing like fresh ocean air to start your day. The yoga deck would be perfect for the class, with the sound of the waves and the seabirds creating a natural soundtrack for healing.

She was adjusting the meditation cushions when she heard footsteps on the front porch. Through the window, she saw Archer standing there, looking like he might run away at any second. He was a full twenty minutes early. She opened the door and offered a warm smile, knowing this was hard for him.

"Good morning. Come on in and get settled."

Archer stepped inside, his movement still stiff and guarded. He wore simple workout clothes like she'd suggested, and his hair was slightly damp from what she guessed was a morning walk on the beach.

"I wasn't sure—" he started, looking around uncertainly.

"You're exactly where you need to be," Luna said.

"Would you like some tea while we wait for the others?"

"Tea would be good," Archer said as he followed her into the kitchen. "Same kind as before?"

Luna nodded, preparing two cups of her abuela's blend. "It helps relax the muscles before we start. My grandmother always said tension lives in our bodies long before it shows up in our minds."

"She sounds like she was a very wise woman with a lot to say," Archer said, chuckling.

"That's probably an accurate representation," Luna responded.

She watched as Archer took a careful sip, noting how his shoulders seemed to lower slightly with each breath.

"So, how many others?" he asked, his voice a bit gruff.

"Just three today. Everyone's working through different injuries or pain. Sarah is recovering from back surgery. I also have a fisherman with a chronic knee issue and a retired teacher with arthritis. So, everyone's journey is different."

Before he could respond, the door opened and the other students began arriving. Luna watched as he retreated slightly into himself, positioning himself at the back of the deck. She understood that he needed space to have the illusion of privacy, even in a group setting. There was probably the worry also that someone would recognize him. She assumed that would be very upsetting.

Once everyone settled in on their mats, she began the class, keeping her voice soft but clear so they could hear it over the waves.

"So we'll start just by breathing," she said. "Nothing fancy, nothing complicated—something that we all know how to do. Just notice how your breath moves through your body. In and out, in and out."

She guided them through general warm-ups, careful to offer modifications for those with different abilities. And when they reached the shoulder exercises, she saw Archer hesitate.

"Remember," she said to the group but met his eyes briefly. "We're not pushing hard today. We're listening. Your body knows exactly what it needs, and our job is to pay attention."

To her surprise, Archer just closed his eyes and followed her instructions. His movements were deliberate and careful. The morning sun caught a little fleck of gold in his hair, and for a moment, she could see past the injured athlete with the bad attitude to the person underneath, someone who was just trying to find his way back to himself.

As the class progressed, she guided them through a series of gentle stretches and movements, keeping her voice steady and calm. She noticed how Archer's breathing gradually deepened, how the tension in his face started to ease. And when they moved to a particularly challenging stretch for the shoulders, she approached him quietly.

"May I?" she asked softly, gesturing to his shoulder.

He nodded slightly, and she made a small adjustment to his position. "Try bringing your elbow down just a bit. Sometimes less movement creates more space."

She felt him jump and stiffen initially at her touch but then slowly relax as the adjustment relieved some pressure. Sarah, at the front of the class, let out a contented sigh as they moved to a gentler pose. The retired teacher, Margaret, smiled in agreement. Even Tom, the fisherman who'd been skeptical about "this kind of thing," seemed to be finding some peace in the movements. But Archer held Luna's attention. There was just something about the way he approached every movement—determined but careful, like he was discovering new parts of his body with every breath.

They moved into the final relaxation pose, and Luna spoke.

"Let your body settle," she instructed softly. "Feel the support of the mat beneath you, the warmth of the sun, the sound of the waves. Right now, there is nothing to fix, nothing to change, nothing to achieve. There's just this moment."

She watched as Archer's fists slowly unclenched, his breathing deepening, and for the first time since she'd met him, he looked at peace.

After class, as the other students gathered their things and chatted quietly, Luna noticed Archer lingering on his mat, his eyes still closed. She tidied up and gave him the space to process whatever he was feeling.

"That was wonderful, dear," Margaret said, touching Luna's arm as she passed. "My joints haven't felt this good in ages."

"Same time Thursday?" Sarah asked, her face more relaxed than when she'd arrived.

Luna nodded, walking them to the door.

Tom paused. "Didn't think this sort of thing would help, but my knee feels better. Who'd have thought?"

After they left, Luna returned to the yoga deck where Archer was finally sitting up, running a hand through his hair.

"How are you feeling?" she asked, keeping her distance.

"Different. I can't explain it, but different."

"Do you want some more tea?"

He nodded, and she moved to the kitchen to

prepare it. They sat out on the deck chairs, looking at the ocean.

"My shoulder," he said as she handed him the tea. "It's not screaming at me for the first time in months."

"That's because we worked with it instead of against it. Sometimes healing starts with acceptance."

He took a sip of the tea. "You make it sound so simple."

"Simple doesn't always mean easy," she replied.

He held up the cup of tea. "I think I might be getting addicted to this."

They sat in comfortable silence for a while, drinking tea and watching the waves. She could feel something had switched in him, but she knew better than to point it out.

"So, will you be at Sunday dinner?" he asked, suddenly surprising her.

"Oh, at SuAnn's? Yes. I'm a little bit worried about her attempts to cook Puerto Rican cuisine, though."

A ghost of a smile crossed his face. "Yeah, Dawson mentioned something about that. Said she'd been practicing all week."

"Well, she called me three times yesterday about plantains. I finally had to promise to come early and help."

Archer turned to look at her. "You know, for someone who grew up with all that—the food, culture, the beauty of Puerto Rico—Seagrove must seem pretty simple in comparison."

"Simple isn't always a bad thing," Luna said. "Sometimes it's exactly what we need. So, will you be there at dinner?"

"Apparently, I don't have a choice. According to Dawson, in this town, with these women—" he trailed off, shaking his head.

"Resistance is futile?"

"Something along those lines."

He stood carefully. "I should go, but Thursday?"

"Same time. We'll be here."

After he left, she finished her tea on the deck and let the morning sun warm her face. She could hear the distant sounds of Seagrove waking up with shop doors opening and cars moving along the beach road. Her abuela had always said that healing happened in its own time, like the tide coming in and out. You couldn't rush it. You couldn't force it. You just had to create the space for it to happen. Her goal was to make space not only for Archer, but for the whole town of Seagrove.

~

Luna made it to SuAnn's house early as promised, following the aroma of spices and garlic up the porch steps. The white clapboard house sat back from the road, surrounded by flowering bushes and old oak trees draped with Spanish moss. She didn't even get a chance to knock before the door swung open.

SuAnn stood there in a floral apron, her face flushed from cooking. "Oh, good Lord, thank goodness you're here. These plantains are giving me fits."

Luna couldn't help but laugh as she followed SuAnn into the bright, warm kitchen. Every surface was covered with ingredients or cooking utensils, and something that smelled suspiciously like sofrito was simmering on the stove.

"Have you been cooking all day?" Luna asked, setting down her bag and rolling up her sleeves.

"Since dawn," SuAnn said. "I'm too old for this, but I just wanted everything to be perfect. It's your first Sunday dinner with us, and, well—" she gestured to all the chaos around her. "I might have gotten a little carried away."

Luna moved to the counter where several plantains sat in various stages of preparation. "These need to be a bit riper for a mofongo," she said gently, "but we can work with what we have. My abuela taught me a few tricks."

As they worked side by side, Luna showed SuAnn how to properly mash the plantains with garlic and olive oil, sharing stories about learning to cook in her grandma's kitchen in Puerto Rico. The kitchen was filled with the familiar scent of her childhood mixed with SuAnn's traditional Southern dishes.

"You know," SuAnn said, leaning against the counter as she watched Luna work. "I've never seen Archer so quiet as he was after that movement class of yours."

Luna's hands stilled for a moment. "First of all, you haven't known Archer any longer than I have. And second of all, he's actually been to two classes. And third of all, it has nothing to do with the two of us getting together or falling in love. He's trying to heal."

"Oh, don't worry, honey. I'm not meddling… much." SuAnn winked. "I just thought you should know that I think what you're doing is making a difference."

Before Luna could respond, they heard voices from the front porch. Sunday dinner was about to begin.

The front door opened, and a rush of voices and laughter came rolling inside. Julie and Dawson arrived first with their son, Dylan, followed by Janine and Dixie, who was wearing a flowing turquoise dress adorned with a seashell pattern.

"Something smells amazing," Dixie said, making her way to the kitchen. She paused for a moment, looking around to take in the scene. "Well, look at this. It's like Puerto Rico met the Lowcountry. I do believe we're in for a treat."

Luna smiled and wiped her hands on a kitchen towel. "SuAnn did most of the work. I just helped with the mofongo."

"Oh, don't let her fool you," SuAnn said, stirring something in a pot on the stove. "This girl knows her way around a kitchen. I can tell that her grand-mother taught her well."

The front door opened again, and Luna's heart raced when she heard Archer's voice in the hallway. He showed up in the kitchen a few moments later, looking surprisingly relaxed in a light blue button-down shirt and khakis.

"You came," Julie said, looking at him and smiling.

"Like you gave me a choice," he said. His eyes met Luna's briefly, and she saw a flicker of something—maybe appreciation—before he looked away.

"Well, don't just stand there," SuAnn said. "Every-body out on the porch. Dinner's ready to be served."

The screened porch was set up with a long table, decorated with fresh flowers and candles. The evening breeze carried the sound of the distant waves, mixing with the salty air and the aromas coming from the kitchen. Luna found herself seated between Dixie and Archer, with SuAnn at the head of the table.

"Where's Harrison?" Julie asked.

"Oh, he's not feeling so well tonight. I promised I'd bring him home some leftovers," Dixie said.

"And where's Nick, by the way?" Dixie asked SuAnn.

"He went to visit some family in Alabama. He'll be back next week. Now, let's get on with Sunday dinner. Luna, honey, you have to tell me whether or not I did your grandmother's recipe justice," SuAnn said as she started passing around the dishes. After realizing SuAnn was serious about cooking, Luna had sent her one of her grandmother's recipes.

"Everything looks wonderful. My abuela would be honored that you wanted to learn any of her recipes. Cooking was her greatest passion."

"The mofongo smells amazing," Julie said, helping herself to a generous portion.

There was a mixture of foods, from Puerto Rican dishes to Lowcountry favorites like cheese grits and peach cobbler. Everybody's plate looked like a mish-mash of cultures. Beside Luna, Archer was oddly quiet, studying the unfamiliar dishes with careful consideration. He was still favoring his shoulder, even with the simple act of passing dishes.

"Try this," Luna said softly, spooning some mofongo onto his plate. "It's plantains mashed with garlic and olive oil—the comfort food of my childhood."

"Your childhood in Puerto Rico?"

"Summers with my grandmother," she explained. "She had this tiny little kitchen that always smelled like sofrito and coffee. She could make anything taste like home."

On her other side, Dixie was regaling the table with stories about Seagrove's history, her bangles jingling as she gestured enthusiastically. But Luna couldn't help but remain aware of Archer beside her, watching as he took his first bite of mofongo.

"This is—" he paused for a moment, searching for words, "really good. Like, really good."

Luna felt a warmth of satisfaction. "Food has a way of bringing people together. My abuela always said a shared meal could heal almost anything."

"She sounds like a smart woman," Dawson said from across the table. "And thanks to SuAnn for hosting all of us here and being willing to try something new," Dawson said, raising his glass of sweet tea. Everyone around the table did the same.

"So, Janine, where's your husband?" Dawson asked, referring to William.

"He had a late marsh tour today, and he didn't want to bail on the people, but I promised him I'd bring home leftovers too. So everybody leave a little bit in the bowls," Janine said, laughing.

"Julie, how are the girls?" Dixie asked, referring to her adult daughters, Colleen and Meg.

"Oh, just busy with their lives. I feel like I don't

get to see them nearly as often as I'd like to. Of course, Meg is still helping out at the bookstore when she gets a chance, but Vivi is always involved in something. She takes ballet now, and she's starting gymnastics classes next week."

"Oh wow, she's getting so big," Dixie said.

"And Colleen?"

"Just being a new mom. You know how exhausting that can be. I invited her and Tucker to come tonight for Sunday dinner, but they just wanted a quiet night in. They did say thank you for the invitation, though," she said to SuAnn.

"Well, I'll see them next week. I'm making a special pound cake to bring over. Being a new mother is very hard."

Luna had always wanted to be a mother, and hearing other people talk about it sometimes tugged at her heartstrings in a way that was hard to explain. It just hadn't been in the cards for her, and now she feared that she was too old to have a child biologically. Of course, to her, it didn't matter. She would do it in any way that she could, but first, she had to find the right man to build a family.

"So, Luna," Dixie said, "you must tell everybody about what happened in your movement class recently. That fisherman, Tom, isn't it? He came into the bookstore and was practically floating."

"Well, sometimes people just need permission to slow down and listen to their bodies. That's all."

"That's not all," Julie said, laughing. "You're creating something very special at Serenity. Everybody can feel it. The whole town's excited."

Much to Luna's relief, the conversation shifted to stories about Seagrove's past. Dixie seemed to have endless tales about the history, each one a little more colorful than the last, but Luna could feel Archer beside her and the way he relaxed—incrementally— as the attention moved away from the classes.

As the evening progressed, the sky turned purple with sunset. Luna found herself feeling more at home here with these relative strangers than she had in years. They were warm and genuine people, and she felt like the town had not been the only thing that had pulled her back to Seagrove after all these years. Maybe God knew that she needed these people, too.

The evening air grew cooler, and SuAnn brought out some coffee and a flan that Luna had helped her prepare earlier. Candles on the table flickered in the breeze.

"This reminds me of the evenings on my abuela's porch," Luna said as she helped serve the dessert. "Though she had these tiny coquí frogs that would sing all night long. Sometimes it was hard to even talk over them."

"Coquí?" Archer asked.

"Oh, they're little tree frogs native to Puerto Rico. They're tiny, but they have this distinct song—co-kee, co-kee—that's how they get their name." Luna smiled, thinking about her grandmother. "My abuela said they sang to remind us that the smallest things can make the biggest impact."

"You mean like gentle movements and breathing?" he asked quietly, his eyes meeting hers.

"Something like that," she said, her cheeks warming.

"Well, it seems like your grandmother had a lot of wisdom," SuAnn said. "And I'm glad to hear her stories and get to share in this Puerto Rican-Southern fusion dinner that I think was a great success."

Everyone smiled and clapped.

"Let me help," Luna said, rising, but SuAnn waved her off.

"No, you cooked. Julie and Janine can help me clean up."

"Spoken like a true mother," Dawson said. "Do you want me to help?" he asked Julie as she stood.

She shook her head and followed her mother and sister into the kitchen. Everyone else helped to clear the table, and Luna found herself sitting with Archer. In the twilight, the strings of light SuAnn had hung around the porch created a soft glow.

"Thank you," he said suddenly.

"For what?"

"For not making a big deal about that class when Dixie brought it up."

"Listen, Archer, your healing journey is your own. It's not for public consumption."

"Yeah, well, you'll find that not much in this town stays private."

"Well, maybe not, but some things can still be sacred. Like healing. Like finding your way back to yourself."

The breeze stirred the Spanish moss in the trees, creating shadows on the porch. She could hear laughter from the kitchen as they cleaned up, SuAnn's voice rising above the rest, although Dixie was a close second.

"You know what's weird?" Archer said after a moment. "My shoulder—it actually felt better after Thursday's class."

"Not just physically, but like something unlocked?" Luna suggested.

"Yeah, and that scares me a little bit."

"Why?"

"Well, because if this helps—if this gentle movement, breathing, and all the stuff I dismissed actually helps—then what does that say about everything I thought I knew? About how I've been approaching my recovery this whole time?"

"It says you're brave enough to try something new, Archer. That's all it has to say right now. It doesn't have to mean anything big."

Their eyes met in the soft porch light, and Luna felt something shift, a subtle change in the air, like that moment before it starts raining.

"More coffee out here?" Julie broke the tension as she stepped onto the porch with a fresh pot.

"Oh, no thanks," Archer said, standing carefully. "I need to head out. Early morning tomorrow."

"Another class?" Julie asked.

"Maybe," Archer said. "Thanks for dinner and for, well, everything."

After he left, Julie settled into his vacated chair. "Well?"

"Don't—" Luna warned.

"I didn't say anything."

"Yeah, well, you were thinking it very loudly."

Julie laughed. "Can you blame me? That's the most I've heard him say at one time since he came back to Seagrove."

Luna watched the spot where Archer had disappeared into the darkness. "You know, he's trying. That's what really matters."

CHAPTER 7

Archer arrived early for his next movement class, finding the door already open. He would never admit it to Luna, but he was starting to enjoy this. Any kind of structure was good for him. For so many years, he'd spent every single morning on the golf course. He knew exactly what each day would hold. He had a very regimented schedule, and until he started these movement classes, he didn't remember how important that was to him. It was helping his mood more than he would have expected.

He heard Luna's voice drifting from inside as she spoke with another student—Sarah, the woman he remembered from last time. She and her daughter were only visiting for a week, so as far as he knew, this was going to be her last class. He hesitated at the threshold, watching Luna demonstrate a gentle stretch.

There was something about the way she moved—confident but gentle. It made his chest tighten in an unfamiliar way.

"Good morning," Luna said when she noticed him. Her smile was warm, but she was professional as she finished up with Sarah.

Archer nodded and moved to his spot at the back of the deck. He was not one of those guys who wanted to be in the front of the class, unless he was really good at something. He unrolled his mat and caught himself watching Luna's reflection in the window—the way she moved through the space, the quiet authority in her movements, the gentle strength in her hands as she adjusted Sarah's form.

Other students filtered in—Tom with his knee issue and Margaret with her arthritis. Luna started the class.

"Remember what we learned last time about listening to our bodies?"

Archer closed his eyes and followed her instructions. Today felt different, easier. His shoulder felt looser, more cooperative, but that familiar drive to push harder kicked in. When Luna demonstrated a variation of their usual shoulder stretch, he automatically went all in and reached for it.

"Careful," Luna's voice said quietly beside him.

He hadn't noticed that she was there because his eyes were closed.

"Remember what we talked about?"

He opened his eyes and found her kneeling next to his mat, her expression concerned. He could see flecks of gold in her dark eyes that he hadn't noticed before.

"But I can do it," he insisted, pushing further into the stretch.

But then something in his shoulder caught and sent a sharp pain down his arm. He dropped the position, frustration building in his throat.

Luna touched his arm briefly—so briefly he thought he may have imagined it. "Start again," she said softly, "and remember, sometimes moving backward is the way forward."

Archer forced himself to release the tension and start over again with the basic movement. He would have to be okay with not doing the more advanced move for now. Luna stayed beside him for a moment longer than necessary, and he found himself oddly aware of her presence, the subtle scent of something floral that he couldn't name.

"That's better," she said quietly before she moved on to help Margaret, who seemed to be completely lost.

He watched her go, noting how all the other students responded to her and her kindness. They trusted her—you could see it on their faces. They relaxed under her guidance. He'd seen that kind of trust before, but it was usually reserved for coaches who had proven themselves through championships and victories. But Luna earned it differently— through gentle persistence and a quiet under- standing.

The rest of the class passed in a blur of careful movements and focused breathing, but when Luna led them through the final relaxation, Archer found his thoughts not drifting to golf today or even his injury, but to Sunday dinner. The way she had defended his privacy and understood his silence.

When class was over and the others gathered their things and left, he lingered. He told himself it was because he wanted to stretch a little more, but he knew he was waiting for something else—some time with her.

"You know, you pushed too hard today," Luna said, kneeling to straighten some cushions near his mat.

"Old habits."

"Die hard?" she asked as she glanced at him.

"Something like that."

He sat up, watching as she moved around the space like she'd been doing this forever.

"Does it get easier? Not pushing so hard?"

She paused. "It gets different. You learn to push in new ways, toward different things."

Their eyes met, and something unspoken passed between them. Archer found himself wanting to ask her more about her journey here, about how she'd learned these lessons herself, but the moment was broken by Tom returning to retrieve his forgotten water bottle.

"I should go," Archer said, although he made no move to leave.

"Yeah, I've got a therapy client coming in about an hour. But how's the shoulder?" Luna asked.

"It's—" he rotated it carefully. "Actually better, even after pushing too hard. I don't understand it."

"Maybe you don't need to understand everything, Archer. Maybe just accept that better is enough for now."

He watched as she gathered her teaching notes, struck by how different she was from his physical therapists and doctors. They all wanted to explain everything, map out every detail of recovery, but Luna just let things be.

"Sunday dinner was nice."

She looked up, surprised. "It was. SuAnn's already planning the next one, of course. This time she wants to try her hand at Japanese food, but I told her I really can't help her out there."

He laughed. "Of course, she's already planning it."

He stood, wincing slightly. "This town doesn't do anything halfway, does it?"

"Oh, says the man who just tried to push himself too far in a gentle movement class," she said, accenting the word *gentle*.

Their eyes met, and Archer felt the corner of his mouth twitch. "Touché."

Luna smiled, and this wasn't her professional smile. It was something quieter, sweeter, more real. For a moment, they just stood there with unspoken words, but then the chime of Luna's phone broke the silence.

"Ah, it's my client wanting to know if she can come early."

"I won't hold you up," Archer said, walking toward the front door.

"See you next time?" she asked as he headed outside.

He nodded, not trusting himself to say anything more. But as he left Serenity, he found himself already looking forward to the next class, and he knew it had absolutely nothing to do with his shoulder.

～

Julie organized a shipment of books on a new release shelf at Down Yonder, while Dawson sat in one of the oversized armchairs nearby. He was supposed to be helping, but he seemed to mostly watch her work.

"You know, you're staring again," Julie said without looking up.

"Can't help it. You're cute when you're in librarian mode."

She laughed and tucked a strand of her hair behind her ear. "You know, I'm trying to get these displayed before my writing group shows up. My editor has also been breathing down my neck about my next book deadline. I promised I'd have the file over to her next week."

"Speaking of watching people," Dawson said, trying to get her off the topic of work so she was less stressed out. "I saw Archer leaving Serenity this morning after another class, and you know what he looked like? Peaceful."

Julie paused. "Peaceful? Hmm, that must have really been something. Luna's good for him. She sees past all of his defenses."

"You mean like you did with me?"

"Oh, you didn't have nearly as many walls as Archer does," Julie said, sitting on the arm of his chair. "I think I had way more walls than you did. A terrible, cheating ex-husband, two grown daughters, and a lot of heartbreak."

He pulled her into his lap. "I wasn't going to let you get away."

"And now look at you," she said, laughing, "married to a romance author who runs a bookstore. An energetic little boy. Running an inn together. Life's crazy, huh?"

"Speaking of romance," he nodded toward the window where he could see Luna walking past, carrying fresh flowers from the florist.

"They'd be perfect together," Julie said, "if Archer would just let himself heal."

"Give them time. Some people take a scenic route to happiness."

Julie turned to face him. "We sure didn't. We were together from the moment we met each other."

He laughed. "Well, again, I wasn't going to let you get away. I've never met a woman like you. I was just a contractor with a bunch of sawdust in my pockets and a closed inn. I knew what I had, and I was going to fight for it."

"Well, I appreciate that, honey, because the man I had before you certainly didn't," she said softly. "And you're the best thing that has ever happened to me."

"And you," Dawson said, brushing a kiss against her temple, "are the best thing that's ever happened to me and this town. You help everybody. You run the bookstore, write your own books, and you make everyone feel welcome in the process."

"*We* make them feel welcome," Julie corrected, "and that's what I love about us. We're partners in everything. I never had that before."

She didn't like to bring up her ex-husband, Michael, that often. She couldn't even remember the last time she'd heard where he was or what was going on in his life. He didn't have a relationship with his daughters anymore, and she knew that probably hurt them, but Dawson had stood in the gap, and they loved him with everything they had.

Dawson looked down at the stack of papers in Julie's briefcase against the chair - her latest manuscript. "And even if I'm just a guy who brings you coffee when you're up late, you'll still love me?"

"Especially then," she smiled. "You know, between the store, the writing, and all the town events, sometimes I worry I'm spreading myself too thin."

"Well, you're amazing at all of it."

"But I never want to take us for granted," she said. "I see how Luna looks at life, like every moment is precious and every chance for a connection is important. It reminds me to slow down sometimes."

"Speaking of connections," Dawson nodded again toward the window where he could now see Archer walking past.

"He's so different around her," Julie said. "More present."

"Yeah, like he's waking up," Dawson agreed. "Reminds me of someone else who needed a second chance at happiness."

She squeezed his hand. "Everyone deserves that chance. Sometimes they just need a little help seeing it."

"Or a lot of help in Archer's case," Dawson said, chuckling.

"Good thing we're experts at helping people find their happy endings," Julie said, standing up. "Now, help me with these books before my writing group arrives."

Dawson stood, pulling her close for a moment. "I love you, you know that?"

"I know," Julie smiled. "I love you too, even when you try to distract me from my work."

"Especially then," he echoed her earlier words, reaching for a stack of books.

Luna prepared for her first meditation workshop. The morning had brought a steady stream of curious locals, some enthusiastic and others clearly skeptical but willing to try something new. She was adjusting the last cushion when a movement caught her eye. Archer stood at the edge of the property, pretending to stretch but clearly watching. Their eyes met briefly, and then he looked away, focusing on the ocean.

"First time doing a group meditation?" Margaret asked as she sat on one of the cushions.

"In Seagrove, yes," Luna said, trying not to be obvious about her awareness that Archer was standing nearby. "I used to lead them all the time in Austin."

More participants arrived, a mix of tourists and locals. Tom, the fisherman, was there once again. As much as he complained, he seemed to be enjoying the process. Luna began the session, guiding them through some basic breathing exercises, but she noticed that Archer had moved a little closer, now leaning against a nearby tree.

"Let's start by finding our center," she said, her voice steady. "Sometimes the hardest part of meditation is just allowing ourselves to be still."

Through the session, she kept catching glimpses of Archer's reactions—the way he unconsciously matched their breathing patterns, how his stance would gradually relax. When she talked about finding peace in the stillness, his expression shifted to something more thoughtful.

"When we resist stillness," Luna continued, "we often resist healing. Our minds want to stay busy, to keep moving, because movement feels like progress."

She watched as her students settled deeper into their meditation. Even Tom, who had declared himself to "not be the sitting still type," had found a moment of peace.

"But sometimes," she said softly, "the biggest changes happen to us in the quiet moments. The moments when we finally stop pushing so hard and realize that progress can be found in the stillness."

She didn't look at Archer, but she felt his attention on her. From her peripheral vision, she saw him push away from the tree and walk a few steps closer to the deck.

As the session continued, the sound of the waves provided a natural rhythm to their breathing. When Luna finally brought them back to awareness, the group seemed reluctant to even break their peaceful silence.

"Well, that was different," Tom said, standing slowly, "but a good different."

Luna answered questions, scheduled private sessions, and watched her students leave. When she turned back to where Archer had been standing, he was gone.

Later, as she prepared for her afternoon clients, she heard footsteps on the deck. Archer was standing in the doorway.

"Those breathing techniques," he said, without any preamble. "Do they really help? I mean, with pain?"

Luna met his eyes. "They can. Would you like to learn some?"

He waited a moment, hesitating, an internal struggle playing across his face. "Maybe, if you have time."

"I always have time to help people with their healing." She gestured to a quiet corner on the deck. "We can start now if you'd like."

He hesitantly moved toward the space. "I don't need a whole session. Maybe just show me the basics, and I can take it from there."

"Oh, of course," Luna said, keeping her voice neutral, professional, although her pulse quickened at his proximity. Why did he smell so good? What was that cologne?

"Let's start with something simple." She demonstrated a basic breathing pattern, watching as he attempted to follow. "So you're going to breathe in through your nose for four counts. Hold your breath for seven counts. Purse your lips and blow out for eight counts."

He tried it a couple of times but seemed very tense.

"May I?" she asked, gesturing toward his posture. He nodded, and she moved behind him, her hands

111

hovering near but not touching his shoulders. "So imagine releasing the weight you're carrying and letting your shoulders drop naturally."

"Easier said than done."

"I know." She stepped around to face him. "But that's why we practice. Try again."

Their eyes met, and something shifted in his expression, a softening around the hard edges. He nodded, closing his eyes. This time, his breath came deeper, more natural, and Luna watched the tension ease from his face. She caught herself memorizing the strong line of his jaw and the way his hair fell across his forehead.

"Better. Actually, much better."

"How often?" Archer asked when he opened his eyes.

"Whenever you need it. That's the beauty of breathing. You can do it whenever. It's always available to you."

"So it's that simple?" he asked, skepticism on his face.

"Simple doesn't mean easy," she reminded him. "But yes, it's that simple."

"When the pain comes, when you start to feel frustrated—"

"When I want to grab a golf club and pretend nothing's wrong?" The vulnerability in his voice caught her off guard.

"Especially then."

"Thank you for this. For not making it a whole thing."

"You don't have to explain. I understand."

"Yeah, I'm starting to believe you do."

The moment stretched between them until the door opened and Luna's next clients started wandering in.

"Oh, I should go," he said, backing toward the door. "I'll see you Thursday."

"I'll always be here."

CHAPTER 8

Luna finished with her last therapy client of the day. It was only a little after two o'clock, and she was happy to have some free time. Maybe she would get some laundry done or make some phone calls. There were still some things around the house that she needed to get done, like a new front flower bed and a spot that needed to be repainted on the outside. There was always something to do, and being a single woman meant she had to do it all. And as much as she wished that she had had children, she was kind of glad in these moments that she didn't have to care for somebody else while just trying to take care of herself.

"Have you ever been kayaking?"

She was startled to see Archer standing in the

front doorway after her last client left. She had apparently left the door open.

"Archer, you scared me to death," she said, putting her hand on her chest as she walked toward the door. "And to answer your question—not since college. Why?"

"Because you've been in Seagrove for weeks and you haven't even seen the marsh yet. It's a real crime if you ask me."

"And so you came here to offer a remedy to this situation?"

"Well, you can consider it payback for all the breathing lessons," he said, laughing under his breath. "I mean, unless you're too busy."

She looked at her schedule and then back at Archer, knowing full well there was nothing on it for the rest of the day. But did she want to go kayaking in the marsh or did she want to do laundry? That was a sad question to even ask herself.

"I'm not too busy, though I should warn you— although I went kayaking, I wasn't exactly graceful at it."

"Well, then, it's a good thing I'm an excellent teacher, I suppose."

His smile was genuine and caught her off guard. It didn't have its usual edge of pain.

An hour later, they stood at the edge of the

marsh. Archer showed her how to settle into the kayak, his hands steady and sure as he helped her find her balance.

"Ready?" he asked, pushing off in his kayak.

She nodded and followed his lead into the quiet waterway. The afternoon sun had painted every-thing in a soft gold, and birds called overhead. It was very different from the ocean's constant motion. Here, everything moved more slowly. The water looked like glass, with only their kayaks breaking it.

"This is beautiful," she said as she watched a heron lift off from nearby reeds.

"Yeah, it's a different kind of peace than the beach," Archer said. "I like to come out here when the ocean feels a little too much."

She understood what he meant. The ocean demanded your attention, but the marsh invited quiet reflection. They paddled in comfortable silence, following the natural curves of the marsh.

"You're a natural at this," he said, guiding them into a quieter channel.

"My father would disagree. He tried to teach me how to canoe once. I think I was twelve years old. It didn't end well."

"No?" Archer slowed his kayak, turning to face her.

"Yeah, we ended up in the water. I lost his

favorite fishing hat." She smiled at the memory. "He wasn't angry with me, just disappointed, and I think that was almost worse."

"Sounds familiar," Archer said. "My dad was the same way about golf. Well, at least in the beginning."

They watched a pair of egrets take flight.

"So do you think that's why you pushed yourself so hard? To avoid disappointing him?"

He was quiet for so long that she thought maybe he wasn't going to answer the question.

"I guess maybe I just didn't know how to be anything else."

"I get that," Luna said. "You know, after my divorce, I had to figure out who I was without being someone's wife, or someone's therapist, or someone's daughter. Just—who was Luna by herself?"

His paddle stilled. "I didn't know you were married before."

"Yeah, it was very brief, right out of grad school. He was a surgeon, a very focused guy, super driven—just like I was back then." She guided her kayak around a bend. "And when things fell apart, I threw myself into work. I thought if I could fix enough other people's problems, maybe I would fix my own."

"So you thought you could fix yourself by fixing other people?"

"Yeah, something like that."

"And did it? The helping others—did it fix things?"

"Not exactly." Luna watched the ripples spread across the water from her paddle. "It just kept me busy enough so I didn't have to notice just how empty everything else felt. And then my grandmother got sick."

He guided them toward a small inlet where the water opened into a peaceful lagoon.

"Your grandmother from Puerto Rico?"

"No, my father's mother—the one who left me the inheritance for Serenity. She used to say I was trying so hard to heal everyone else I had forgotten how to heal myself."

"Sounds like you had two really awesome grandmothers."

"I did. And when Grammy got sick, I finally slowed down enough to listen—to breathe. Kind of like what you're doing now."

Archer's paddle dipped into the water, creating a tiny whirlpool. "I'm not very good at it yet."

"Neither was I. I'm still not sometimes."

"So is that why you came here to Seagrove? To heal?"

"Partly, but also partly because I wanted to create something real, something that mattered. You know, in Austin, everything for me was about appearances, but here, I feel more honest—more like that version of myself I've been trying to find. I've been chasing the feeling I got in Seagrove as a little kid for my entire life."

"Well, there's no pretending in Seagrove. Trust me, I've tried. Nobody around here will allow it."

The sun was starting to lower, casting long shadows across the marsh grass. They paddled back through the marsh, the setting sun painting the sky in shades of orange and pink. Luna felt a sense of peace, and it was a feeling she'd been chasing for longer than she cared to admit.

"Thank you for this," she said, "for showing me another side of Seagrove I didn't even know about."

He guided his kayak alongside hers. "Well, thank you for trusting me to show it to you."

They pulled their kayaks onto the bank and then gathered their things. Luna couldn't help but notice just how comfortable it was to do things with Archer.

"Same time next week?" Archer asked as they walked back.

"Are you suggesting we make this a regular thing?"

"Maybe," he shrugged. "Everyone needs a break from the ocean sometimes."

"Even you?"

"Especially me. I'm learning it's okay to need

things, and maybe even to want things—other than a golf club."

"So you think you need or want to kayak with me on the marsh?"

"Maybe both." His gaze held hers for a long moment before he finally looked away. "I should get going. I've got a very early session with the physical therapist tomorrow."

"Of course. I'll see you in class soon."

"Wouldn't miss it."

As she walked back to Serenity, Luna couldn't shake the feeling that something had fundamentally changed between them. She had shared pieces of her past and seen glimpses of his, and they had crossed some invisible line. She wasn't sure what waited on the other side.

Luna stood on the porch and watched storm clouds gather over the ocean. The air had a heaviness about it, and it definitely signaled some rain coming. In the distance, she watched the seagulls zip around in the sky, but their usual lazy circles were replaced by urgent flight.

"Storm's coming," Dixie said when she appeared beside her with a stack of books. "Weather report says it's going to be a big one."

Luna nodded. "Yeah, I've never felt wind like this before, and I've never been on the coast when a storm happened. Any advice?"

"Well, you just want to batten down the hatches, as they say." Dixie gestured toward the beach. "Secure anything that could blow away, stock up on supplies, and hunker down until it passes."

Luna thought of the large windows and the delicate wind chimes on the yoga deck. "Well, I'd better get started then."

"Want some help?" Dixie asked. "Many hands make light work."

"I'd love some," Luna said, grateful for the offer. "I was planning on asking SuAnn and Julie to come over and help me, too."

"Oh, they'll be here. You know, SuAnn's probably already baking up a storm, getting ready to feed everybody in town," Dixie chuckled. "That woman has never met a crisis that she didn't think a casserole could fix."

Luna laughed. She loved having Dixie around. She knew that Dixie had Parkinson's, as did her husband, but you would never know it. She acted like nothing was wrong and played tennis several times a week.

As if on cue, SuAnn's car pulled up, followed closely by Julie's. They both jumped out, their arms laden with bags.

"We come bearing supplies," Julie announced. "I've got you some flashlights, batteries, and enough of Mama's comfort food to last a good week."

"Y'all are lifesavers," Luna said.

They set to work securing the outdoor furniture, checking the flashlights, and filling water jugs. As they worked, the wind continued to rise, the first drops of rain coming with it. By late afternoon, Serenity was as ready as it was going to be. The large windows were shuttered, the yoga deck was cleared of anything that could take flight, candles stood at the ready, and SuAnn's food filled the refrigerator.

"Well, I think that's everything," Julie said, wiping her hands on the front of her jeans. "We should be all set to ride it out. It's not going to be as big as some of the ones we've had before, but you're a newbie here, so we wanted you to feel comfortable. And if you don't want to stay here, you can definitely come to my house or stay at my mom's."

"Oh no, I don't need to do that. I appreciate it, though."

"That's what community is for," SuAnn said, pulling her into a hug. "We take care of each other around here."

A loud crack of thunder made them all jump, and rain started lashing against the shutters, the wind howling around the eaves.

"Well, looks like it's here," Dixie said, peering out a crack in the shutters. "Gonna be a wild night."

"And you're sure you don't want to come stay with one of us?" Julie asked. "Might be safer than staying out here alone, although the inn is right on the beach as well. We're just a little bit further back than you are."

Luna hesitated. Part of her did want to accept the offer, to surround herself with the comfort of company, but she had grown used to being alone in all kinds of situations, and this was no different.

"I appreciate it," she said, "but I think I need to be here, prove to myself that I can weather the storm, so to speak."

"I get it. But you call us if you need anything, okay? Anything at all," Julie said.

They all hugged each other and promised to check in when the storm was over, and Luna found herself alone, listening to the storm rage outside. She lit a few candles, made herself a cup of her grandmother's tea, and settled in to wait it out.

Luna sat by the window with a blanket wrapped around her shoulders and watched as the wind whirled past her. The wind was so strong that it seemed like it was going to blow her away right along with the house.

The power had gone out over an hour ago, which left Serenity lit by only candlelight and the occasional flash of lightning. Luna was so happy that she had bought some of those candles that are battery-powered, and she had plenty of them in her drawer. In the flickering shadows, she found herself thinking about her own life. How many storms had she weathered over her years? The tempest of her parents' divorce, the whirlwind of her own short-lived failed marriage, and then the long years that she'd spent longing to make a family with someone and just not finding the right person.

Each time, she'd thought she'd found shelter in someone, but ended up being disappointed. So, she'd kept busy helping others, trying to desperately outrun her own pain.

She never dealt with it until recently. Just like the makeshift shutters that were rattling against the windows during the storm, all of those moments had been only temporary. And that is why she had come to Seagrove—not just to start something new, but to learn how to withstand the storm and find her own solid ground.

She thought about Archer and how he had shared pieces of his own struggle when they were kayaking. He seemed to be tentatively, slowly learning to breathe through the pain instead of pushing and fighting against it. And wasn't that what she was doing now in her own way? Learning to be present in the discomfort of not getting the very things she had wanted her whole life. Learning how to find peace in the midst of this tempest.

A particularly loud crack of thunder made her jump. She laughed softly at herself and shook her head. "Yeah, some meditation teacher I am. I can't believe I just got startled by a little thunder."

She thought about how she wanted someone to share Serenity with her. Maybe she would get a little dog since she was allergic to cats. She'd seen the animal shelter driving into town and made a mental note to visit there soon.

As she settled back against the cushions, she felt a sense of calm wash over her. There was a storm raging outside, no doubt about it. Yes, she was sitting alone in the dark, but she was here in Seagrove. She was breathing, and somehow, right now, that was enough.

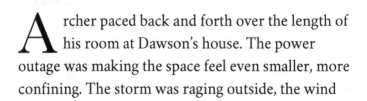

Archer paced back and forth over the length of his room at Dawson's house. The power outage was making the space feel even smaller, more confining. The storm was raging outside, the wind howling and the rain lashing against the windows. It had been many years since he'd seen a storm like this. He'd never minded them growing up. He found a strange comfort in the chaos and enjoyed the wild, untamed energy of the South Carolina Lowcountry during a storm.

But tonight, he felt restless. He was almost at the edge of worry. He couldn't help himself—his thoughts kept circling back to Luna. The way he'd seen Serenity's shuttered windows when he walked back down the beach, evidence of her preparations. The image of her there alone in the sprawling house nagged at him. He knew she was more than capable. She had a quiet strength that most people only dreamed of having.

But he wasn't sure what to call this thing developing between them. Maybe he was imagining it. Maybe he was leaning on her a little too much. But it didn't stop the concern gnawing at his gut. Before he could even second-guess himself, he grabbed his rain jacket and headed for the door. But when he opened it, the wind nearly knocked him off his feet as he stepped outside. Rain pelted him in the face like tiny daggers, cold and sharp. He squinted into the darkness, trying to orient himself toward Serenity.

What was he doing? Only an idiot would walk on the beach in the middle of this kind of storm. He was one of those people who would be on the news for dying in a silly way, like being impaled by a palm tree or knocked to the ground by a flying dolphin.

Luna was fine. She had to be. And even if she wasn't, what could he possibly offer her? A guy with a bum shoulder was going to save her? He was still trying to figure out how to navigate his own storms. But for some reason, his feet just kept moving, propelling him down the beach.

Underneath the worry and the uncertainty was the truth he was beginning to acknowledge. He wanted to be there with Luna—not just for her, but for himself.

When he reached Serenity's porch, rain streaming down his face, he raised his hand to knock and hesitated. What if she didn't want him there? What if she didn't want to be stuck inside with one of her clients during a storm? What if he was overstepping?

But then, faintly over the howl of the wind, he heard something—the soft strains of music, the gentle chords of a guitar. And then, he realized he was exactly where he was meant to be.

He knocked, the sound almost lost to the roar of the storm. For a long moment, there was no response, and then the door cracked open. All he could see was Luna's surprised face in the candlelight. Man, she was even more beautiful in candlelight.

"Archer? What are you doing here?" Her eyes were wide as she took in his drenched appearance. "Is everything okay? Are Julie and Dawson—"

"Yeah, I just—" He ran his hand through his wet hair, suddenly feeling like a fool. "I wanted to make sure you were all right with the storms and all."

In that moment, he realized he could have just called her and asked if that's all he wanted. It would have been easy to send her a text and ask if she was okay. He knew that, and she knew that, and now he was exposed. Now she knew he just wanted to be there with her, and he didn't even know exactly why.

Something softened in her expression. "That's really sweet of you. Come in, you must be freezing to death."

She stepped aside and ushered him into the warmth of Serenity. His face was transformed by candlelight, with shadows dancing on the walls. The soft music he'd heard from the porch wrapped around them. He stripped off his raincoat and hung it on the coat rack by the door.

"I didn't know you played," he said, pointing toward a guitar leaning against the couch.

She smiled just a little. "It helps me feel grounded, especially in moments like this."

She motioned for him to sit and handed him a

towel. "I was about to make some tea. Would you like some?"

"Oh, tea sounds perfect." His adrenaline was starting to settle down.

Luna busied herself in the kitchen, and Archer looked around the room. Despite the storm raging outside, the place was peaceful. There was a steadiness that seemed to always emanate from Luna herself.

She returned with two steaming mugs, handing him one before sitting on the couch.

"So, you braved a hurricane to check on me?"

"Uh, it wasn't quite a hurricane, just a bad storm, and it seemed like the right thing to do. I mean, you're new here."

"Well, I appreciate it more than you know." Her eyes met his, candlelight flickering in their depths. "You know, it's been a long time since somebody's done something like that for me. I can't remember the last time someone cared where I was."

The unspoken weight of her words hung in the air, and Archer found himself wanting to know more, wanting to know all of her stories.

He cradled his mug, letting the warmth seep into his hands. "You know, I'm not great at this," he admitted, his voice low. "The whole being there for someone thing. I've been pretty self-centered for a long time."

"I think we've all been there. It's easy to get lost in our own storms."

"How do you do it?" he asked, genuinely curious. "Stay so steady, even in the midst of all this chaos?"

She traced the rim of the mug with her fingers, considering his question. "You know, I guess I've learned that the only way out of chaos is by going through it. That sometimes the only thing we can do is just breathe and be present—not run away, even when everything around us is falling apart."

He'd been learning that in her classes—that strength wasn't about pushing harder, but about yielding to what was and getting through it.

"I'm starting to see that," he said softly, "though I'm not always good at it, as you can tell."

"We're all just practicing every single day. Life is one long practice. None of us ever master it." She set her mug down and picked up the guitar. "When I'm struggling, music helps. It gives me something to focus on, something I can channel all of that restless energy into."

She began to play a soft, haunting melody that seemed to weave itself into the rain. He watched her, mesmerized. There was just something so intimate about seeing her like this, lost in the music and unguarded. She closed her eyes and swayed like he wasn't there, and it was one of the most vulnerable and strong things he'd ever seen.

The last notes faded away, and she looked up, meeting his gaze.

"Luna—" he trailed off, unsure of how to put whatever he was feeling into words.

She seemed to understand and set the guitar aside as she reached for his hand. It felt like an anchor in the storm. It felt like a lifeline, a tether to something real. Archer found himself tracing small circles on her palm with his thumb, marveling at the softness of her skin.

"I'm glad you're here," Luna whispered. "I didn't realize how much I needed this until now."

"Me too," Archer admitted. "I've been so used to weathering storms alone all these years that I forgot how good it can feel to have someone beside me."

Luna's eyes met his. "We all need reminders sometimes that we're not alone, even when it feels like we are."

Suddenly, she leaned in and rested her head on his shoulder. Archer's breath caught at the way her body seemed to fit so naturally against his. He let his cheek rest against her hair, breathing in the smell of strawberries and something that was just uniquely Luna. Suddenly, he felt like he had just come home.

They sat like that for a long time, just listening to the rain and the wind, drawing comfort from each other, and Archer felt his muscles loosening, the knot of tension he'd been carrying for years falling away.

When Luna finally sat up, she had a softness in her eyes. "Thank you," she said, "for being here. For caring."

He reached up and brushed a strand of hair from her face, and his fingers lingered on her cheek.

"Anytime."

Outside, the storm continued to rage, but inside, in the cocoon of candlelight and shared understanding, they had found a different kind of peace.

CHAPTER 9

T he morning after the storm was bright and
clear with a blue sky. Archer had gone home
after the rain had stopped. Actually, it was in the wee
hours of the morning, Luna supposed.

They drank tea, talked about life, and spent way
too much time looking into each other's eyes. She
didn't know what was going on, and she couldn't
think about it this morning. She was slightly embar-
rassed, to be honest. She had never become so close
to a client, and it certainly was not something she
intended to do.

Of course, Archer was not working with her for
therapy. He was using her services to learn about
yoga and breathing and meditation, but the lines
were still blurry in her eyes. Being a professional
therapist, she shouldn't have let it go so far to where

she put her head on his shoulder. What was she thinking?

Either way, she had more important things to focus on when she stepped out onto Serenity's porch and surveyed the damage. Tree branches littered the yard, and debris from the beach had washed up nearly to the steps. But she noticed something even more important—the signs of the community coming together. She could see neighbors out in force, clearing branches and checking on each other.

"Luna!" Julie called, waving from the road. She was wearing work gloves and had a determined expression on her face. "Are you okay? How's Serenity?"

"Still standing," Luna said, smiling. "Just needs a little cleanup. How did the inn do? And Down Yonder?"

"Same. We were lucky on both counts, but some of the shops on Main Street got hit pretty hard. We're all heading over there to help out. Are you in?"

Luna nodded. "Yeah, let me go grab my gloves, and I'll be there in a few minutes."

She turned back inside and nearly collided with Archer, who was somehow already at her house and carrying a stack of fallen shutters.

"Whoa, easy there."

"Sorry," Luna said, steadying herself with his arm. "I didn't know you had come back over here. I guess

I'm in a little bit of a hurry to get over to Main Street. Julie said it's all hands on deck."

"Then what are we waiting for? Let's go."

They walked together to the heart of town, joining the throng of residents already hard at work. Luna saw SuAnn directing traffic, a tray of sandwiches in hand. Dixie was helping sweep up glass from a broken storefront along with her husband. She was wearing one of her usual colorful outfits with hot pink capri pants and a white t-shirt that had a sequined flamingo on the front.

Luna and Archer jumped right in, helping in the efforts to clear debris and salvage what they could from the damaged shops. Luna also got to meet some people she hadn't yet met. Janine's husband, William, who ran marsh tours in town, introduced himself, as did both of Julie's daughters, Colleen and Meg. Colleen had a brand-new baby, so she wasn't able to help out too much, although she did have the baby attached to her in a sling, while her husband, Tucker, helped hang an awning that had fallen down in the winds. Meg's husband, Christian, helped corral their daughter most of the time, while Meg handed out food with her grandmother.

Luna couldn't believe how the community had come together so quickly, like they were one big family. Archer and Luna worked in tandem easily. They hauled a waterlogged bench out of the florist's shop, and Luna couldn't help but marvel at the way everyone had rallied so quickly. Nobody was a stranger today. They were just neighbors, friends, and a community united.

"Quite a sight, isn't it?" Archer said, as if he could read her mind. He nodded toward where Tom, the once-gruff fisherman from class, was replanting flowers alongside others in the community.

"This is amazing. I've never seen anything like it. Everybody came together so quickly. I mean, they're already planting flowers," Luna said.

"That's Seagrove for you. We take care of our own."

Luna smiled. "We? So are you calling Seagrove your home again?"

He shrugged his shoulders. "I don't know. I wouldn't say that, necessarily. I don't really know what the future holds at this point, but right now, Seagrove is my hometown. Always will be."

The sun started beating overhead, and it seemed like the storm from the night before hadn't even happened. They all worked through the morning, pausing only to eat sandwiches and lemonade from SuAnn's seemingly endless supply. By afternoon, Main Street was looking a lot more like itself—a bit battered but not broken.

As they surveyed their handiwork, Archer put his

arm around Luna's shoulders unexpectedly, a gesture that made her heart literally flutter.

"Not bad for a day's work," he said, squeezing her gently.

She leaned in a little too much, savoring the warmth of his presence. "Yeah, not bad at all."

Around them, the town came back to life. Shopkeepers swept their stoops, and neighbors made plans for shared dinner meals as children chased each other through the streets. Seagrove, once again, had proven itself unshakable.

Standing there, surrounded by the hum of neighbors chatting, Luna realized that she had proven herself unshakable, too. With Archer by her side and this community at her back, she felt ready to weather whatever storms might come. And the fact that she was even thinking that way scared her.

Archer stood at the first tee, his hands holding the club like a lifeline. The familiar green expanse stretched out before him, but today it felt like a battlefield instead of a playground.

"Are you ready?" Luna asked softly from beside him.

He looked over at her. When she'd offered to come with him today to guide him through some breathing techniques they'd been practicing, he'd been hesitant at first. The golf course had always been his sanctuary. It was a place where he could escape the craziness of the world and focus just on the game. Bringing Luna into that space felt like a risk, like he was exposing a part of himself that he liked to keep hidden. But as he stood there, he felt the tension coiling in his shoulders like a rattlesnake. He knew he needed her steady presence more than he ever did.

"As ready as I'll ever be," he said, trying to sound lighthearted even though he didn't feel that way.

She nodded and stepped back to give him space. "Now remember, it's not about the score today. It's about finding that peaceful connection again, that joy in the game."

He took a deep breath and focused on the word joy. When was the last time he felt that on the course? Golf had always been about perfection, about pushing himself to be better, faster, stronger. But now, with the injury and the weight of uncertainty pressing down on him, he had to find joy in a different way.

He set up his shot, feeling the old familiar motions come back to him. As he drew the club back, he felt the twinge in his shoulder and his breath hitched, signaling pain.

"Breathe," Luna murmured from behind him, "just like we practiced."

He closed his eyes and focused on the rhythm of his breath—in and out, slow and steady. He pictured the tension flowing out of him like water, leaving his body. As he exhaled, he swung and felt the club connect with the ball in a satisfying thwack. The ball soared down the fairway. It certainly wasn't his farthest drive ever, but it was straighter and truer than he'd managed in months. He couldn't help himself and felt a grin tug at his lips.

"Beautiful!" Luna said. When he turned to her, he could see the pride in her eyes. "How did that feel?"

"Like a beginning," he said. "Like maybe there's still a place for me out here after all."

She reached out, her hand finding his. "There will always be a place for you, Archer. On the course, in Seagrove, and in my life."

The words hung between them. He felt his throat tighten. What did that mean, exactly?

"Thank you," he managed to say, squeezing her hand, "for being here, for believing in me."

"Always," Luna said softly. "Now, let's see what other magic we can make out here today."

They made their way down the fairway, and Archer felt a different kind of hope taking root inside of him. With Luna by his side, he felt like he could conquer the world. Like he could face anything, even the uncertain future that still stretched out before him.

~

Archer stood on the driving range and watched as a group of kids gathered around him. They all looked so eager and excited, and it reminded him of when he was a kid and started golfing with his dad.

When he'd first mentioned the idea of giving some free lessons to local youth, Dawson jumped into action. He was enthusiastic about everything. If he had to describe Dawson to somebody else, it would be a golden retriever. He was always at the ready and excited for whatever was to come.

Dawson also saw the idea of giving lessons as a sign of growth in Archer. He always saw the best in him. Some of the country club members had been skeptical, wondering what a former golfer would gain from teaching a bunch of scrappy Seagrove kids. But Archer looked out at the crew assembled before him and felt a sense of rightness in his bones. Right now, this is where he was meant to be, sharing his love of the game with a new generation.

"Okay, everybody," he said, clapping his hands to

get their attention. "Who's ready to learn how to swing like a pro?"

A chorus of excited cheers went up from the kids. He smiled, feeling their enthusiasm wash over him like a medicine.

"Okay, first things first," he said, picking up a club. "Your grip. If you don't start with the right grip, everything else about your game is going to fall apart."

He showed them the proper hand placement and then moved through the group, adjusting fingers and offering critiques and encouragement. As he worked, he couldn't help but be excited about the way the kids were soaking up his instructions, their faces lighting up with determination. It was a whole different side of the game he'd never witnessed himself. He was that kid back in those days, and then he went on to be a professional. He was only worried about himself, but now he was feeling joy from these children.

Had he ever been quite as eager and hungry to learn as they were? He tried to remember back to his early days, but all he remembered was the pressure of tournaments and sponsorships that eventually weighed him down.

"Coach Archer, do you mean like this?" One of the boys, a pretty scrawny kid with a mop full of red hair, held up his club.

Archer crouched down and made a small adjustment. "Perfect, you're a natural, kid."

The boy smiled, puffing up with pride. Archer felt warmth in his chest. This is what he'd been missing, this pure love of the game, untainted by any expectations or competition or ego. As the lesson progressed, he found himself lost in the rhythm of teaching, laughing and chatting with the kids. And for the first time in longer than he could remember, he didn't feel the pain in his shoulder. It must have been there somewhere in the background, but it was being overpowered by joy and satisfaction.

"Looks like you've got quite the fan club."

Archer turned and saw Luna standing at the edge of the range. He felt his heart flip over in his chest.

"What can I say?" he said, trying to act nonchalant. "I'm always a hit with the under-twelve crowd."

"Yeah, I probably wouldn't go around saying things like that in public," Luna said, laughing. "Seriously though, this is wonderful. Look at how happy they are."

Archer looked over at the kids as they grinned and chatted with each other, each of them practicing their grip. "You know, I didn't realize how much I needed this," he said softly, "to remember what it's like to just love something for the sake of loving it."

She touched his arm. "Well, sometimes the greatest gifts come in unexpected packages."

"Thank you for encouraging me to do this, for always seeing something in me that I can't see in myself."

"You've always had it in you, Archer. You just needed a little reminder of who you are beneath all the accolades and expectations."

As the day wound to a close and Luna headed back to Serenity, Archer held on to the feeling—the love for the game, the joy of sharing it with others, and the support of this woman he'd been lucky enough to meet.

L una spread out a blanket on the sand, watching as Archer unpacked the picnic basket he'd brought. The evening air was warm, as it often was in the South Carolina Lowcountry, and carried with it the salty-sweet scent of the ocean. She'd never expected this. Hadn't expected him to suggest that they share dinner on the beach after her last class of the day.

"All right, SuAnn insisted on providing the food," he said, pulling out the containers. "I don't want you to think I'm lying about being a good cook or something. It's definitely not my forte. But I think she's convinced that we're both too busy to eat properly."

Luna smiled, thinking of SuAnn's motherly

concern. "You know, she's not wrong. Most days I forget about lunch entirely."

"Well, that stops now," Archer said, his tone mock-serious. "Coach's orders."

"Ah, Coach?" Luna raised an eyebrow. "So I see the kids at the golf course are rubbing off on you."

"They're good kids, eager to learn, with no agenda except the pure joy of hitting that ball really far. I'm trying to remember back when I felt the same way. When competition wasn't a thing and I was just competing with myself."

Luna watched him arrange the food and noticed that his movements were getting more fluid by the day. He was way less guarded with his physical movement.

"You know, you're different when you talk about teaching."

"Different how?"

"I don't know, more at peace, maybe? Like you found something you didn't know you were looking for."

Their eyes met briefly before Archer looked away, opening a container. "Well, maybe I have."

They ate in comfortable silence, watching the waves roll in. Luna couldn't help but steal glances at him, watching how the light played across his features and how, when he was around her, the tension in him seemed to lift.

"Tell me something," he finally said. "Something I don't know about you."

Luna considered the question, pulling her knees up to her chest. "Well, I used to be afraid of the ocean."

"You? But you're always talking about its healing properties."

"Well, that came later. But when I was little, after my parents split up, I would always have these dreams about drowning. It took me years before I would even put my feet in the water."

"What changed?"

"My abuela. She taught me that sometimes things that we fear the most are the things that will save us." She smiled at the memory. "Anyway, she would stand in the waves with me in Puerto Rico when I would visit and hold my hand and teach me to breathe with the rhythm of the water."

He was quiet for a moment. "Like you're teaching me to breathe through the pain."

"I guess so," Luna said softly. "We all need someone to stand in the waves with us sometimes."

The sun started to sink behind the horizon, casting the sky in hues of orange and pink.

"Do you ever miss Austin?" Archer asked.

"Sometimes, but not in the way you might think. I mean, I miss knowing where everything is and all of the familiarity of that, but I don't miss who I was when I was living there."

"And who were you there?"

"I was somebody who was always running, trying to fix everyone else so I wouldn't have to look too closely at my own broken pieces." She drew patterns in the sand beside the blanket absentmindedly. "Here I can just be. I can be whoever Luna is that day."

He nodded. "I get that. Before my injury, I was always chasing the next tournament, the next win. And I guess I thought if I won the next thing, I would feel something change inside of me. But I never really had time to stop and think about what I really wanted. And now..." He trailed off. "I am learning that maybe the things worth having aren't ones that you have to chase."

The words hung between them.

"You know, the kids at your lessons seem to understand that instinctively."

"Kids do," he agreed. "Most kids, anyway. They don't have all the pressure or expectations. They just follow joy without guilt or reservation."

A cool breeze swept in from the ocean, making her shiver slightly. Archer reached over for his jacket but then seemed to catch himself, remembering that there was still a professional boundary between them, she supposed.

"Well, we should probably head back," Luna said. "Early class tomorrow."

"Right," Archer said, helping her pack up. "Thanks for sharing dinner with me and telling me the story about your grandmother."

"Thanks for asking," Luna said, smiling.

CHAPTER 10

Luna sat cross-legged on Serenity's deck with Janine after their morning yoga session. Everyone else had left, leaving them alone with their hot tea and the rhythm of the waves in the background.

"You're a bit quieter than usual," Janine said. "Still thinking about that romantic beach picnic with Archer?"

Luna looked up quickly. "Wait, how did you—"

"Small town, remember? Besides, I saw you two out there," she said, smiling. "You looked very comfortable together."

"Yeah, too comfortable, maybe." Luna traced the rim of her cup with her index finger. "Janine, I can't afford to blur those lines. He's still technically my client. What if I get a reputation for getting romantically involved with clients? That's terrible."

"Is he your client, though? I mean, when was the last time he came to an actual, formal session?"

Luna thought about it. The movement classes had evolved into something less structured. Their conversations had shifted from therapeutic to something else entirely.

"It's too complicated," Luna said.

"Yeah, well, life usually is." Janine shifted and faced Luna. "Can I be honest with you?"

"Of course."

"I see the way you two look at each other. Like, both of you are afraid to take that first step and terrified of what happens if you don't."

"I came here to build something, Janine, to create a place of healing. I can't risk that for—for what? Love?"

The word hung between them like a weighted blanket.

"The last time I risked everything for love," Luna said quietly, "I ended up having to start over completely."

"Yeah, and look what happened when you started over. You found Seagrove. You found yourself. So maybe sometimes starting over isn't an ending. It's an opening."

Luna watched a pair of seagulls chasing each

other across the morning sky. "I'm scared, Janine, not just of getting hurt, but of hurting him. He's been through so much already."

"You know what I think?" Janine said, leaning back. "I think you're both so used to taking care of everybody else that you've forgotten how to let someone take care of you."

She wasn't wrong. Luna thought about all her years of counseling and how the whole time she kept her own heart carefully guarded and didn't really let anyone in. And then Archer, who had pushed through the pain to maintain his image—neither one of them was very good at letting others in.

"But what if it doesn't work?" Luna asked. "What if we ruin everything? This friendship, this progress he's made, my place, and my name in Seagrove."

"And what if it does work?" Janine said. "What if it's exactly why you both ended up here? Sometimes the universe has a funny way of bringing people together at exactly the right moment. What if you waste that opportunity?"

Luna smiled. "Now you sound like Dixie."

"Worse people to sound like," Janine said, standing and gathering her yoga mat. "Look, just don't let fear make your decisions for you, Luna. You've spent your whole life teaching others to be brave. Maybe it's time to take some of your own advice."

Archer stared at the email on his phone, reading it for the third time. He couldn't believe it. The prestigious Oakland Hills Golf Academy in California wanted him as their head junior coach. He would have full benefits, a huge salary, and the chance to work with some of the country's most promising young golfers. A month ago, he wouldn't have even considered something like this. He had only wanted to go back to professional golfing or sit around and sulk for the rest of his life, but working with the kids in Seagrove had made him open to the possibility. And now he thought of it as a way to stay connected to the game he loved without the pressure of competition.

But now, as he looked out the window of his room at the inn, he could see Serenity. Luna would be finishing her morning class about now. He pictured her moving through the space with the quiet grace that she always had. Luna was true serenity to him.

His phone buzzed, another email from Oakland Hills requesting a response or asking if he had any questions, wanting to meet with him. They needed an answer within the week. A knock on the door interrupted his thoughts.

"Come in."

"Hey, got a minute?" Dawson asked, leaning against the doorframe. "Julie sent me up with coffee, but I really think she wanted me to check on you. She said you looked a little troubled at breakfast."

Archer held up his phone. "I got a job offer. Oakland Hills Golf Academy."

Dawson's eyebrows shot up. "Wait, is that in California?"

"Yeah, a long way from Seagrove," Archer said.

"Yeah. Have you told Luna?"

The question hit him like a physical blow. "Well, no, not yet. I mean, I don't know how to. She's got her whole life here now. She's just starting here. Serenity is thriving and she's making a real difference. I don't want to mess things up between us."

"Well, I'm pretty sure that ship has sailed, my friend. You have to tell her."

Archer stood and paced to the window. "You know, maybe it's better this way. It'll be a clean break before things get too complicated."

"I think it's too late for that," Dawson said. "Question is, what do you really want?"

Archer wished he knew the answer. "What do I want? I want to stay in the game. I want to make a difference. But I also want..." He trailed off, not finishing his sentence, the truth of all of it catching in his throat.

"Luna," Dawson finished.

"Yeah, well, it's not that simple."

"Actually, it is that simple. We just like to complicate things too much," Dawson said, sitting down in the armchair. "You know, when I met Julie, we were both scared. She had been hurt and I'd been alone for a long time. I had other opportunities that would have taken me out of Seagrove. Job offers."

"You never told me that."

"Because it wasn't important. The moment I got those job offers, I realized I couldn't imagine my life without Julie. And that decision made itself. I never even told her about them."

He leaned forward, his elbows resting on his knees. "The thing is, Archer, you're not the same person who would have jumped at this offer six months ago."

"No, I'm not."

"Those kids that you're teaching here, that life you're building—you have to decide, is it worth it for you to give it up for some prestigious title and big salary all the way in California?"

"I need to think about it," he said finally.

"Well, just don't think so hard you miss what's right in front of you." Dawson stood and started walking toward the door, setting down a cup of coffee on his way. "And Archer, you know, you shouldn't wait too long to tell her. News gets around in Seagrove."

"Hey, please don't tell anybody, even Julie. I need some time to think."

"Of course, man, I would never tell anyone."

After Dawson left, Archer sat on his bed, the weight of the decision pressing down on him. His phone buzzed again—another email from Oakland Hills offering him some times to Zoom. They obviously wanted him. He understood why. He had a big reputation in the golf world. But did that even matter to him anymore? He needed to make a choice, but he just wished he knew which one was right.

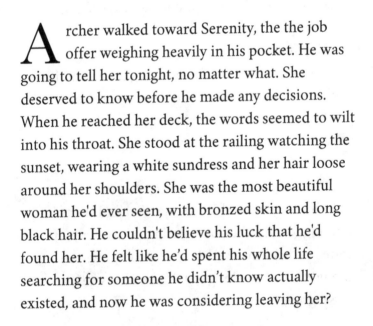

Archer walked toward Serenity, the the job offer weighing heavily in his pocket. He was going to tell her tonight, no matter what. She deserved to know before he made any decisions. When he reached her deck, the words seemed to wilt into his throat. She stood at the railing watching the sunset, wearing a white sundress and her hair loose around her shoulders. She was the most beautiful woman he'd ever seen, with bronzed skin and long black hair. He couldn't believe his luck that he'd found her. He felt like he'd spent his whole life searching for someone he didn't know actually existed, and now he was considering leaving her?

She turned at his approach, and her smile hit him like a physical force. "Perfect timing," she said. "I was just thinking about how we talked the other day about finding joy in the simple moments."

He joined her at the railing, close enough to catch the scent of her perfume. "Oh yeah?"

"So I thought maybe," she hesitated, "well maybe you would like to have dinner with me tomorrow night. Not on the beach this time. There's a little place in town I've been wanting to try."

His heart thumped in his chest. Did she just ask him on a date? The job offer pressed against his leg, reminding him why he'd come there. He should tell her. He should tell her right now before things got too complicated. But instead, he heard himself say, "I'd love that."

She smiled and then turned back to the sunset. He found himself leaning closer, drawn to her by some invisible force. A car door slammed somewhere nearby, breaking the spell. Luna stepped back, but her smile remained. "So tomorrow then?"

"Tomorrow," he said. Words about California burning in his throat. He would tell her at dinner. He promised himself. As he watched her walk back inside, he wondered if he was already in too deep.

～

Luna stood in front of her mirror, smoothing her sundress. When she had asked Archer to dinner at The Blue Crab, she had tried to tell herself this couldn't really be a date, but the butterflies in her stomach suggested otherwise.

The knock at the door made her heart jump. She found Archer on her porch, wearing khakis and a pink button-down shirt that brought out the blue in his eyes. He looked different somehow, less guarded.

"Hi," she said softly.

"Hi." He cleared his throat. "You look beyond beautiful."

Luna felt warmth creep up into her cheeks. "Well, you clean up pretty good yourself."

They walked to the restaurant in the evening air. Luna was aware of Archer right beside her, and the way their arms brushed against each other with each step. The Blue Crab sat right on the water, its deck strung with twinkly lights. Their table overlooked the marsh, and they could see fishing boats off in the distance.

"I've been wanting to try this place since I got to town," Luna said. "Julie says they have the best seafood in town."

"They do," Archer agreed. "They've been around since I was a kid, but don't tell SuAnn I said they have the best seafood. She swears her crab cakes are the best in town. SuAnn has quite a competitive streak when it comes to food."

Luna laughed, feeling some of the nervousness ease. This was still Archer, the same man who had become her friend and an important part of her life, but tonight felt different.

Their conversation flowed easily over dinner, moving from stories about Archer's golf students to Luna's latest classes. She also talked a lot about growing up and visiting Puerto Rico, while Archer told some stories about Dawson and him that made her laugh. She found herself watching his face as he talked, noticing how the corners of his eyes crinkled when he smiled.

"Speaking of golf," he said, setting down his fork, "there was something I wanted to ask you."

"Oh?"

"Well, the Seagrove Golf Classic is coming up next weekend. I wasn't going to go, but I'm feeling a little better about it now and I'd like to attend. It's an annual charity tournament, pretty big deal around here." He paused and looked like he was gathering his courage. "I was wondering if you might be my date for the tournament and for the dinner dance after."

Luna felt a warmth in her chest. "A tournament and a dance? That's quite an invitation."

"Too much?"

"No," she said, "not too much at all. Actually, I'd love to come."

"Great, that's great," he said, a smile breaking across his face. "Though I should warn you, I'm not much of a dancer."

"Well, I'm not much of a golfer, so I guess we're even."

"Well, we could fix that, you know. I could teach you some basics before the tournament, if you want."

Luna thought about being close to him. "I'd like that."

The waiter appeared with dessert menus, breaking the moment between them.

"SuAnn will never forgive us if we don't try the key lime pie," Archer said. "It's the only dessert in town that she admits is better than her own."

"Well, we wouldn't want to disappoint SuAnn."

They shared a slice, and Luna found herself hyper-aware of his every movement—the way his fingers brushed against hers as he passed her a napkin, or how his eyes lingered on her face when she took her first bite.

"Verdict?" he asked.

"Amazing, though again, I don't think we should tell SuAnn that I said that."

He laughed, and it wrapped around her like a warm summer breeze.

When they finished dessert, the restaurant's

lights dimmed slightly, and soft music drifted from the hidden speakers.

"You want to walk on the beach before heading back?" Archer asked. "It's beautiful at night, as you know."

She nodded.

They strolled along the beach, close, but not quite touching. The moon cast silver ribbons across the water.

"Thank you for dinner," Luna said. "I invited you, so you didn't have to pay for it. And also, thanks for inviting me to the tournament."

"Well, thank you for saying yes," he said to both.

They walked back to Serenity, both aware that something had changed, even if neither one of them was ready to name it yet.

L una stood on the practice green right at sunrise, watching Archer as he set up for their impromptu lesson. The morning air was crisp, which was unusual in the Lowcountry, so she was enjoying it. It carried with it the scent of freshly cut grass.

"Okay, the first rule of golf," Archer said, handing her a club, "is grip. Everything else builds from there."

Luna took the club and tried to mimic the way she had seen him hold it. Archer shook his head, moving in to stand behind her.

"May I?" he asked softly.

She nodded, and he stepped closer, his chest barely brushing her back as he reached around to adjust her hands on the club. She couldn't help but feel her heart speed up at his proximity and the gentle way he positioned her fingers.

"Like this," he said, his breath warm against her ear. "Left hand here, right hand here. You feel how they work together?"

"Yes," Luna said, trying to make sure her voice didn't shake. She was acutely aware of him, the solid warmth of his presence, and the faint scent of his aftershave.

"Now, for the stance." Archer stepped back slightly, and Luna felt a loss. "Feet shoulder-width apart, knees slightly bent."

She followed his instructions and tried to focus on the mechanics of what he was teaching her, rather than the way his eyes followed her every move.

"Good," he said. "Now we're ready for the swing. Remember how we talked about breathing in class? Well, it's the same kind of thing here. It's all about the rhythm and allowing your body to move naturally."

He demonstrated the motion, and Luna watched the fluid grace of his swing, the way his shoulders seemed to cooperate today instead of fighting him.

"Now your turn," he said, moving behind her again. "No pressure, nice and easy."

Luna took a deep breath and tried to concentrate on the mechanics, but it was really hard. Archer was a very good-looking man, and he smelled like heaven. How was she supposed to figure out how to swing this golf club when she couldn't stop thinking about his breath against her ear?

She drew the club back and attempted to mirror his fluid motion.

"Wait," he said softly. She hadn't noticed that he was there because her eyes were closed. "You're too tense right here." His hand moved over her shoulder. "Remember what we practice in class. Let the tension flow out. You're a pro at this."

Luna closed her eyes for a moment, focusing on her breathing. When she opened them, Archer was now at her side.

"Try again," he said. "This time, feel the rhythm of it like the ocean. There's power, but there's also grace."

She swung again. This time, the club connected with the ball and sent it rolling across the practice green. It didn't go very far, but it was straight.

"Beautiful," Archer said.

When she looked at him, she wasn't sure if he was talking about the shot or something else.

"Well, I had a good teacher," she said.

Their eyes met, and for a moment, she felt like the early morning air was electrified. He cleared his throat and stepped back slightly.

"Are you ready to try another?"

Luna nodded, already missing how close he had been to her just moments before.

As the sun climbed higher in the sky, they worked through different shots. His instruction was focused but gentle, and she found herself stealing glances at him, noting how natural he looked out there, how at peace.

"You're very different on the course," she said when they were taking a break.

"Different how?"

"More yourself, maybe? Like you can breathe here?"

His eyes met hers.

"I am. Breathing, I mean. For the first time in a long time."

She felt the weight of his words, understanding that they meant more than just the physical act of breathing. She'd seen such a transformation in him over the past weeks, from the angry, injured man who had first walked into Serenity to this version of

Archer, who could find such joy in teaching children.

"Your turn again," he said, setting up another ball. "Now let's work on that follow-through."

She took her stance, and he moved behind her again, his hands light on her hips.

"Now rotate here," he said softly. "Let your body follow the motion naturally."

She tried to focus on the technical aspects of the swing, but she just couldn't help the way she felt like she needed to turn around and kiss him square on the lips. Probably inappropriate for a golf lesson.

"That's it," he said as she completed another swing. "See? You're a natural."

"Now you're just being kind," she said, laughing and turning to face him.

"I'm being honest," he said.

He was close enough that she could see flecks of green in his eyes and the slight stubble on his jaw. For a moment, neither of them moved. All she could hear was the distant crashing of waves and the sound of birds overhead. She felt herself sway slightly toward him, drawn by some invisible force. But then a groundskeeper's cart rumbled in the distance and broke the spell.

Archer stepped back, running his hand through his hair.

"You know, we should probably wrap up. You've got morning classes to teach."

She nodded, trying to push down the flutter of disappointment she felt.

"Thanks for the lesson."

"Thanks for letting me share this with you," he said softly.

As they walked back toward their cars, Luna realized that somewhere between the breathing exercises and the golf swings, something had shifted between them. She wasn't sure either of them was ready to acknowledge it yet.

CHAPTER 11

"You're overthinking this," Janine said as she watched Luna examine herself in the boutique's mirror for the umpteenth time. The blue dress she wore caught the light beautifully, but Luna's expression remained uncertain.

"You know, I just want to look…" Luna trailed off as she smoothed the fabric with her hands.

"Like you haven't spent hours and hours choosing the perfect dress," Janine said, laughing. "How was that golf lesson, by the way?"

Luna's cheeks heated up. "Well, it was instructional."

Janine handed her another dress that was a soft sage green color. "And did this instruction involve any hands-on teaching?"

"Janine," Luna said, waving her hand.

RACHEL HANNA

"What? I'm just asking what everybody in town is wondering. The way that you two look at each other is like a proposal is going to happen at any moment."

Luna walked into the dressing room, mainly to hide her reddened cheeks and grateful for a moment to compose herself. "There's nothing to wonder about. We're just friends. He's being nice."

"Nice?" Janine's laugh floated over the door. "Archer Hawk isn't being nice. He's either all in or all out, and he watches you when you're teaching class, and he lights up when you're around. That's not just being nice."

Luna slipped the green dress over her head. The fabric settled around her. And when she stepped out, Janine fell silent.

"Oh," Janine said with her hand over her mouth. "That's the one."

Luna turned and looked in the mirror. The dress was simple but elegant, with a subtle shimmer that looked like sea glass. She felt completely sophisticated and totally herself.

"He won't know what hit him," Janine said.

"That's not at all what I'm trying to do," Luna protested, but she was quite sure that her voice lacked all the conviction in the world.

"Isn't it?" Janine said, meeting her eyes in the mirror. "Luna, when are you just going to admit that

166

what's happening between you and Archer is more than friendship?"

Luna sank into one of the plush chairs in the boutique, still wearing the green dress. "I cannot let myself think that way, Janine. There's just too much at stake."

"Like what?"

"Like Serenity. Like his recovery. Like... like my heart."

Janine sat beside her and took one of her hands. "You know what I think? I think you're scared because this is way too real. This thing with Archer, it's... it's not like it was with your ex-husband, where everything was all planned and proper. This thing is unexpected and messy and absolutely genuine."

Luna thought about the morning golf lesson and how her skin had tingled where he touched her, but how natural it felt to have all those moments with him.

"He makes me forget to be careful with my heart," she admitted softly.

"Well, that might be exactly what you need. You came to Seagrove to help others, but maybe you're also here to help yourself learn to be happy."

Luna stood and looked in the mirror again. "This green one," she said finally. "It feels right."

"Like someone else we know," Janine teased.

Luna smiled and allowed her heart to flutter at

the thought of Archer seeing her in this dress and dancing with him under the stars.

Archer stood in front of the mirror, adjusting his tie for the third time. The golf classic had been part of his life for many years before he left Seagrove, but this was his first time as a participant and a junior coach. Today felt different because Luna would be there.

"You're going to wear out that tie if you don't stop fiddling with it," Dawson said in the doorway.

"Why are you always creeping around my room?" Archer joked.

"I don't have anything else to do," Dawson said sheepishly. "I finished the to-do list Julie left me this morning."

"I just want everything to be perfect," Archer said, turning to face his friend. "Those kids have been practicing hard for the exhibition."

"Right, the kids. That's what you're so nervous about," Dawson said with a knowing smile.

Archer wanted to throw something at him. "It has nothing to do with a certain therapist in a new dress."

Archer's hand went to his pocket, where that email

from Oakland Hills felt like it was burning a hole. He should have already told Luna. It had been too long now. He should have just been honest before even asking her on this date, before letting himself fall.

"You still haven't told her," Dawson suddenly said. It wasn't a question.

"I will after the tournament. I just don't want to ruin today."

"Archer—"

"I know, okay? I know I'm making it worse by waiting, and she's going to be really upset with me, but you should have seen her lately. The way she lights up when she talks about Serenity, about building a life here. How am I supposed to tell her I might be leaving? And why do I even assume that she'll care? Maybe I'm just a client to her."

Dawson leaned against the doorframe. "You're not just worried about telling her about the job, are you?"

"What do you mean?"

"I mean, you're falling for her. Hard. Actually, I think you've already fallen, and that scares you more than any career decision."

Archer looked back in the mirror. He wasn't seeing his own reflection. He was seeing Luna on the practice green at sunrise. The way she trusted him to guide her. The way she felt in his arms. The way she made him feel whole again—not like just some broken athlete trying to find his way back.

"I can't lose her, Dawson," he admitted quietly. "But I also can't ask her to wait for me either. California is a long way from Seagrove."

"Have you considered that maybe you don't want to go?"

Before Archer could respond, his phone buzzed. A text from one of his young students, excited about the exhibition with some final questions. The enthusiasm of the kid brought a smile to his face.

"They're good kids," Dawson said. "And you're great with them—better than you've ever been on the pro circuit, if you ask me."

"They remind me why I fell in love with the game in the first place," Archer said, straightening his tie one more time. "Before it became about money and rankings and sponsorships."

"And Luna? What does she remind you of?"

Archer met Dawson's eyes in the mirror. "That sometimes the best things in life are the ones you never even saw coming."

"Well, you're going to have to make a decision soon. That Oakland Hills offer won't wait forever."

"I know. They gave me another week, so I was grateful for that."

Archer checked his watch. "Well, it's almost time

to head to the course. I just need to get through today."

"And then what? Just keep pretending nothing's changing? And then one day Luna just never sees you again? That's not fair, and you know it."

The truth of Dawson's words hit hard. Nothing about this whole situation was fair—not to Luna, not to his new students in Seagrove, and not really even to himself. But every time he thought about telling her, he just couldn't do it. His stomach turned in knots.

A knock at the door saved him from responding.

Julie appeared, looking elegant in a beautiful summer dress. "The kids are already at the course, Archer, and they're asking for their coach."

Their coach. Not a fallen pro. Not the guy who lost everything. But their coach.

"Go on," Dawson said. "But, Archer—don't wait too long. Some things are worth fighting for."

As Archer drove to the course, he thought about Luna and the way she'd looked at him during their golf lesson. The way she'd helped him find his way back to the game he loved and the person he was inside. Through her gentle understanding, she had changed his whole life.

He pulled into the parking lot. Luna was standing near the clubhouse, and he was blown away by her natural beauty, both inside and out. He felt like his heart stopped, like he might actually need a defibrillator, and then started again with a different rhythm entirely.

***

Archer stood on the practice green, surrounded by his students, with their youthful energy buzzing around him like an electric current. He moved easily between them, adjusting grips, offering encouragement, and celebrating their small victories with a warmth that felt effortless.

"He's different with them, isn't he?" Julie's voice came from beside Luna. She turned to see her friend watching Archer with a knowing smile.

"More like himself somehow," Luna admitted, unable to take her eyes off him. "Even though I've only known him for a few weeks."

A small girl with braids—Jasmine—sank a long putt, and Archer's face lit up with pride. The way he crouched to give her a high-five. The way he encouraged every single child without an ounce of ego or pressure. It was unlike anything Luna had seen in him before.

"They don't see him as a pro golfer or an injured athlete," Luna said softly. "They just see him as somebody who believes in them."

"Kind of like how he sees you," Julie said.

Luna's cheeks warmed. "Julie, you're as bad as your sister."

Julie laughed. "I'm just saying what everyone can see. The way you two look at each other when you think no one's watching? You're not fooling anybody."

Before Luna could respond, Archer looked up and caught her gaze. A slow smile played at his lips, and for a moment, everything else faded. One of the kids called his name, breaking the spell, and he turned back to his students.

"You look beautiful, by the way," Julie said. "Your sundress is adorable. Janine said you picked a gorgeous dress for tonight, too."

Luna smoothed the floral fabric self-consciously. "Your sister helped me pick it out."

"Well, based on the way Archer keeps looking at you, I'd say it was a good choice."

The exhibition match began, and Archer's students eagerly showed off their skills. Luna was enchanted by their enthusiasm, their pure joy in playing a game that had nothing to do with pressure or expectations.

"Coach Archer, watch this!" Jasmine called, lining up another putt. Her face scrunched in concentration.

Archer crouched beside her, his voice steady and encouraging. "Remember what we practiced? Nice and smooth, just like the ocean."

Luna's heart squeezed as she recognized her own advice in his words, adapted into his teaching.

Jasmine took a deep breath, just like Archer had taught her, and tapped the ball. It rolled straight into the cup.

"Did you see that?" she beamed.

Archer grinned, high-fiving her. "Perfect form, Jasmine. Your mom's going to be so proud."

Luna watched as the little girl ran off, practically bouncing with pride, and she felt her chest tighten with something bittersweet. Seeing Archer like this, watching the way he poured himself into teaching, only reminded her that she might not have much more time with him.

Archer looked her way again, and this time, his smile held something more—something that sent a shiver down her spine. He said something to his students before making his way over to her.

"Well, what do you think?" he asked. "Did your breathing techniques help create some future golf pros?"

"I think you did that all on your own," Luna said. "They adore you, you know."

For the briefest moment, something flickered across Archer's face—something like doubt, like hesitation. It was so quick, she almost missed it. But before she could question it, his usual smile returned.

"The tournament's about to start," he said. "You want to walk the course with me?"

"I'd love to," Luna said, then glanced down at her dress. "But first, I need to go change into something more comfortable."

She ran into the clubhouse and changed into a pair of khaki capri pants, a pink golf shirt, and white tennis shoes before meeting Archer near the first tee. She'd put her new dress on later for the dinner and dance.

The tournament had drawn a good crowd, with spectators gathering to watch the local players compete for charity. Everyone greeted Archer with warmth and familiarity—not just as a former pro golfer but as a part of the community. Seagrove had welcomed him back, and in a way, it felt like he'd never left.

"Now you'll have to explain the finer points to me," Luna said as they strolled the fairway. "You know my golf knowledge is still pretty limited despite your excellent teaching skills."

He chuckled. "You're a quick study. Besides, sometimes golf is more about feeling than knowing."

"Like breathing," she said.

"Yep. Just like breathing." His voice was softer now like he wasn't talking about golf at all.

They walked the course together, Archer explaining shots and strategies. Luna listened, but her focus kept shifting to him—the way his whole body relaxed here, the ease in his stride, and the lightness in his voice.

"Coach Archer!" a small voice called out.

Jasmine ran up, still clutching her putter. "Are you gonna dance with Miss Luna at the party tonight?"

Luna felt her face flush as Archer cleared his throat.

"Well, if she'll have me," he said, glancing at Luna.

Luna smiled. "I think that can be arranged."

Jasmine beamed at both of them before her mother called her away, leaving Luna and Archer standing in a moment charged with possibility.

As the tournament wound down, Luna was nervous about the evening ahead. She watched Archer throughout the day, noting how he moved between all of his different roles—coach, community member, and friend. Each facet revealed something about him that made her heart flutter.

"Ready for the next part?" Archer said, appearing beside her as the last players finished. "We have some time to freshen up before the dance."

"Oh, I should probably head home to change then," Luna said.

"So I'll pick you up at seven?"

"Seven," she said.

When she returned to Serenity, she found herself taking extra care of her appearance. She refreshed her makeup, let her dark hair fall in soft waves around her shoulders, and slipped on the green dress that still felt so magical.

At seven o'clock, she heard his car pull up in the driveway. She jumped at the knock as if she wasn't expecting anyone, even though all she was doing was expecting someone.

When she opened the door, Archer's mouth dropped. "Wow, you look stunning."

"Thank you," she said, uncomfortable with the compliment.

"Ready to go?"

"Absolutely."

He reached out his arm, and she interlocked her arm with his as they walked to the car. The drive was a short one, as were most drives in Seagrove. When they arrived, he ran around the car and opened the door for her, and then they walked inside.

The country club ballroom had been transformed with twinkling lights and flowers everywhere. As they entered, Luna felt Archer's hand settle on the small of her back, guiding her through the crowd of people. The simple touch sent electricity through her entire body. Luna already found herself hoping that the night would never end.

They walked around and talked to a few people, including Julie and Dawson, and Janine and her husband, William, before settling at their table. It wasn't long before the band struck up a slow song, and Luna felt Archer shift beside her.

She'd watched him throughout dinner, noticing how he seemed at ease in this familiar setting, but also nervous, stealing glances at her when he thought she wasn't looking. They'd spent the whole time talking to Dixie and her husband, Harrison, as well as SuAnn and Julie's daughters, Colleen and Meg.

Luna enjoyed getting to meet everyone she hadn't met and getting to know others better, but when the slow song came on, all she could think about was Archer sitting next to her.

"Would you like to dance?" he asked softly.

She nodded.

Archer stood and offered his hand, leading her to the dance floor. When he pulled her into his arms, she felt like she couldn't breathe. One of his hands settled on her waist, and the other took hers, and suddenly the rest of the room faded away.

It felt like something from a movie or one of those romance novels she'd read as a kid. She had never really believed that everything around you could disappear when you were with the right person, but that was exactly what was happening.

"I thought you said you weren't much of a dancer," she teased, hoping her racing heart would calm down at some point.

"Well, maybe I just needed the right partner," he said.

He wasn't smiling. His voice was low and obviously only meant for her.

They moved together to the music. Luna found herself drawing closer to him with each step until she could feel the warmth of him through her dress. The scent of his cologne mingled with the evening air, drifting in from the open doors.

"Thanks for coming today," he said, "for watching the kids. For—" His voice suddenly trailed off as his eyes met hers with an intensity that she wasn't expecting.

"I wouldn't have missed it," she replied softly. "Seeing you with them, sharing what you love—it was beautiful."

Something flickered across his face again, just like she had seen before. A joy mixed with something that looked like regret for just a split second, and before she could puzzle it out, he pulled her closer, his cheek brushing against her hair.

Luna just let herself sink into the moment instead of questioning every little thing. She sunk into the gentle sway of their bodies and the warmth of his arms around her.

The music flowed into another slow song, and neither of them made any move to separate.

"You know everyone's watching us," she murmured.

"Let them," Archer said softly. His thumb traced small circles where he held her hand. "I only see you."

Luna's heart stuttered at his words. She lifted her head from where she'd been resting on his shoulder and found his face just inches from hers. His eyes dropped to her lips, and for just a moment, she thought he might kiss her.

But instead, he suddenly drew back slightly, although his arms stayed wrapped around her.

"Want to get some air?"

She nodded, letting him lead her through the French doors onto the terrace. The evening air was soft, and fairy lights twinkled overhead. Music drifted out from the ballroom, but they were alone, finally.

"Tonight has been perfect," Luna said, leaning against the railing like something out of a dream.

Archer stood beside her, close enough that their arms brushed.

"Luna, I—"

But whatever he was about to say was interrupted by Janine appearing in the doorway.

Luna would have to smack her later.

"There you are! They're about to announce the tournament winners!"

Luna felt Archer tense beside her. The moment slipped away like water between their fingers.

They followed Janine back inside, and Luna couldn't help wondering what he had been about to say.

Back inside, Luna found herself hyper-aware of Archer beside her as they listened to the tournament results. His arm would brush hers occasionally, each touch sending sparks through her system. Why was she acting like this? She wasn't in high school, but for some reason, he made her feel giddy. Even her ex-husband had never made her feel that way.

She tried to focus on the announcements, but her mind just kept going back to the moment on the terrace. The way he had looked at her before Janine walked out there—what was he going to say? Was he going to tell her that he was falling in love with her?

The evening started winding down, couples slowly drifting away from the dance floor. Luna still felt so curious as Archer helped her with her wrap.

"Ready to head home?" he asked.

"Of course."

The drive back to Serenity was quiet. There were

lingering glances and lots of unspoken words. When he reached her door, Archer stepped out to walk her to the porch.

She thought very hard about asking him what he was going to say before, but she didn't want to push it. If he wanted to say something, he would have said it. She wished that the night didn't have to end. Maybe she should invite him inside for a cup of tea and some talking. Maybe they would get back to that moment so he could say what he was going to say.

"Thank you," she said, turning to face him. "I mean, for everything. The golf lessons, taking me to the tournament and the dance."

"Luna."

The way he said her name made her breath catch. He stepped closer, and she thought—this is it. This is the moment he's finally going to kiss her.

Instead, he brushed his lips against her cheek, a touch so gentle she thought she might have imagined it.

"Sweet dreams," he whispered.

As she watched him drive away, her cheeks still tingling where his lips had touched, she was more confused than ever.

But she knew one thing for certain.

She couldn't wait to see him again.

CHAPTER 12

L una walked along the beach, which was one of her favorite things to do every day. She was heading toward the inn, hoping to talk to Julie before the bookstore opened. She knew Julie was busy working on her latest book and hoped that she wasn't going to be interrupting anything. It was so beautiful this morning, bright and clear, but her thoughts were unsettled.

Something had been off with Archer since the golf classic. He'd been acting a little strange, and she couldn't tell if he was pulling away or if she had done something to upset him.

As she approached the inn's porch, she heard voices drifting from above. Archer and Dawson, their tones serious despite the early hour.

"Archer, you have to tell her. The Oakland Hills

deadline is coming up. You're just making this harder."

She froze, her heart pounding in her chest.

Archer had explained a lot about golf to her, and one of the things she remembered was a place called Oakland Hills in California.

"I know," Archer's voice was rough. "It's just... every time I try, or I look at her, I think about what I'm leaving behind—"

"It's a prestigious coaching position and a big opportunity," Dawson said. "But California is a long way away."

California.

The word hit Luna like a physical blow.

She pressed her hand against the weathered siding and steadied herself.

"It's my chance to stay in the game," Archer said, "and to make a real difference with young players."

"Well, what about the difference you're making here?" Dawson asked. "With the students here? And with Luna?"

The silence that followed was deafening.

Luna didn't even wait to hear Archer's response. She turned and ran quickly back to Serenity, her vision blurring with tears.

She shouldn't have let herself get so close to a client.

What was she thinking?

Her job was to help him, and now she was upset that he might be leaving.

It wasn't fair to keep him here. Her job was to get people on their feet and moving in the right direction, and maybe California was the right direction for Archer.

But everything made sense now.

His hesitation, the guilty looks that would cross his face like a shadow and then be gone, the way he'd pulled back just when they were getting closer.

He was leaving.

He'd been planning to leave all along.

Luna barely remembered her walk back to Serenity. Her mind was just racing with the fragments of conversation she'd just heard.

A deadline.

Oakland Hills.

California.

She moved through her morning routine mechanically, like she was some kind of robot—lighting candles and trying to prepare for her first class. But her hands trembled, and her chest felt so tight.

"He's leaving," she whispered to an empty room.

The words tasted like ashes in her mouth.

A knock at the door made her jump.

She thought it might be Archer, which was terrifying. She wasn't ready to talk to him.

185

Would she tell him what she overheard?

Or would she let him go without ever knowing that she had heard their conversation?

But instead, she found Janine standing there.

"Luna?" Janine said, her smile fading. "What's wrong?"

The concern in Janine's voice broke something inside of her, and tears spilled over.

"He's leaving," she managed. "Archer—he's been offered some coaching position in California. He's been kind of distant since the golf classic, and I know why now. Why he keeps pulling back. He's known all along that he was going to leave."

Janine crossed the room quickly and pulled Luna into a hug.

"Well, honey, when did he tell you?"

"He didn't tell me." Luna pulled back and wiped her eyes, trying to get cleaned up before her class. "I just overheard him talking to Dawson. He has to make a decision by tomorrow."

"And knowing Archer, he's probably been tying himself up into knots trying to figure out how to tell you."

Luna walked over to the window and looked out at the ocean.

"I've been so stupid, Janine. Letting myself feel things, think things, plan some kind of a future. I was supposed to just be someone helping him. And now look at it. The whole situation is a mess."

"Stop right there," Janine said firmly. "Nothing about what you're feeling is stupid."

"You don't understand," Luna said, turning to look at Janine. "I came here to build something, and to help others heal. I wasn't supposed to—"

She trailed off, wrapping her arms around herself.

"Fall in love?" Janine asked quietly.

Luna closed her eyes against more tears and nodded.

"I can't hold him back, Janine. He deserves this chance to stay in the game he loves and to make a difference on a bigger scale."

"What about what you deserve? What about what he might want?"

"He wants that job. I heard it in his voice." Luna walked over to straighten some books, trying to keep her hands busy and stop herself from crying anymore. "I'm not going to be the reason he gives up his dreams. That was the whole reason why he came here in the first place. I will not be another injury that keeps him from the life he's meant to have."

"Luna?"

"No." Luna straightened her shoulders, pulling in years of practice and professional composure. "I need to step back. I need to make it easier for him to go. And you cannot say anything."

"You're going to make it easier by breaking both of your hearts?"

"I'm going to make it easier by giving him the freedom to choose without guilt."

Luna looked at her watch.

"My first client will be here soon. I need to pull myself together."

"What are you going to do?"

"What I do best," Luna said, forcing a smile. "Help others heal, even if I'm breaking inside."

"You can't just shut down," Janine said. Not after everything you taught us about facing our feelings.

"I'm not shutting down," Luna said. Her voice felt hollow, even to her own ears. "I'm being practical, professional. It's what I should have done all along."

"There's nothing practical about pretending your heart isn't breaking."

Luna paused her straightening of the room. "Well then, what would you have me do, Janine? Beg him to stay? Tell him that in the few months that I've known him, he's become essential?"

Janine said nothing for a moment, then softly replied, "Yes."

Luna turned away. "Look, he needs to make this decision without the complications of worrying about me and my feelings, without me making it harder than it probably already is."

"What about your decision and your feelings?"

"My feelings don't matter, not in this." Luna squared her shoulders, as she had done so many times in her life. "I got to follow my dreams and come here to Seagrove. I cannot ask him to give up his."

A car door slammed outside. Her first client was arriving. Luna took a deep breath.

"Luna," Janine said from the doorway, "just promise me one thing. Don't push him away before he even has a chance to make the choice for himself."

But as Luna prepared to greet her client, she knew she had to do exactly that.

If she didn't start to push him away now, she wasn't sure she would ever be strong enough to let him go when the time came.

It was the worst possible outcome, but she knew what had to be done.

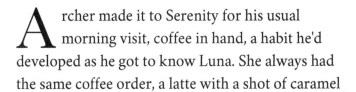

Archer made it to Serenity for his usual morning visit, coffee in hand, a habit he'd developed as he got to know Luna. She always had the same coffee order, a latte with a shot of caramel syrup. But something felt different as soon as he stepped onto the porch.

Through the window, he could see Luna moving around, but she looked stiffer, more controlled—not her usual happy, go-lucky self. When she opened the door, she had a professional smile, not the one she usually gave when she saw him. This was the smile from the first time they met, but it hadn't been directed at him in weeks.

"Archer, I'm sorry, but I have a full schedule today. I won't be able to chat. I'm sorry you wasted time getting those coffees."

He frowned, noting the careful distance she kept between them. "I just thought after the other night—"

"Oh, the other night was lovely," she said, her voice very neutral. "But you know, I've been thinking—I really need to focus on Serenity right now, and on my clients."

"Luna—" He stepped forward, but she moved back slightly.

"I think it's important that we maintain appropriate boundaries," she said, not quite meeting his eyes. "I let things become unprofessional, and that's totally my fault."

"Unprofessional?" His chest tightened. "Is that what you think the other night was?"

"What I think doesn't matter." She finally looked

at him, and there was something in her eyes that made his chest ache. "What matters is that we both have responsibilities and careers to think about."

He felt like he was watching the most precious thing in his life slip right through his fingers. "Did I do something wrong or say something—"

"Oh no," she said quickly. "You didn't do anything wrong. I just… I need some space to think clearly."

He wanted to tell her about Oakland Hills and how torn he felt, and how she had become the most important part of his day. But the words were stuck in his throat, trapped behind the fear of losing her completely.

"Right. Space. Sure." He turned to leave and then paused. "Just tell me one thing—was any of it real, or was I just another project for you to fix?"

The hurt that flashed across her face made him regret the words immediately. But before he could apologize or take them back, she closed the door between them.

He stood on the porch for a long moment after Luna closed the door, the coffees growing cold in his hands. He could see her move to her desk, her back straight, but he caught a slight tremor in her hands as she shuffled papers. He wanted to knock again, to demand answers, to understand what had changed between them since that magical evening on the dance floor.

But her words echoed in his head—appropriate boundaries, unprofessional.

They cut like tiny knives.

If he was one thing, it was a gentleman. There was no way he was going to cross any boundaries she had put up.

The walk back to the inn felt longer than usual. His shoulder ached for the first time in a long time. The Oakland Hills deadline loomed, but instead of clarity, he felt more confused than ever.

"Well, you're back early," Dawson said when Archer walked into the kitchen. "What happened?"

"Luna just shut me out completely." Archer set down the untouched coffees. "Said we needed, and I quote, 'appropriate boundaries', and that she'd let things become unprofessional."

"That doesn't sound like Luna."

"Yeah, no kidding. A few days ago, we were dancing under the twinkle lights, and now she can barely look at me."

Dawson looked at him carefully. "Did you tell her about Oakland Hills?"

"No. I was going to today. She wouldn't even let me in the door."

"Maybe she found out," Dawson said quietly.

"How? I haven't told anybody except you."

"Well, I certainly didn't tell anyone."

Archer sat in the kitchen chair, the weight of the

world pressing down on him. "I've messed this up. By waiting too long to tell her, by letting things develop between us when I knew I might be leaving."

"Or maybe," Dawson said, "you've been looking for reasons to take the Oakland Hills job because you're scared of what's happening between the two of you."

"What's that supposed to mean?"

"It means you spent your whole life chasing the next big thing in golf. But with Luna and with the kids you're teaching, you found something real—something you can't measure in tournament wins or prestigious coaching positions."

Archer couldn't stop thinking about Luna's face when she watched him teach the kids, or about the way she felt in his arms during their dance.

"None of that matters now," he said roughly. "She's made it clear that she wants nothing to do with me."

"Has she?" Dawson challenged. "Or do you think maybe she's protecting herself?"

Archer frowned. "What are you saying?"

Dawson leaned against the counter. "Think about it, Archer. If she did somehow find out about the job offer, what would Luna do?"

"She'd…" Archer trailed off as understanding dawned. "She'd step back. Try to make it easier for me to leave."

"Exactly."

Archer stood and paced the kitchen. "She won't even talk to me. And the Oakland Hills deadline is tomorrow."

"So make a decision," Dawson said. "The real decision—not the one you think you should make."

"You know it's not that simple."

"It actually is." Dawson crossed his arms. "When you think about your future, what do you see? Some big coaching position across the country? Or the life you've started building here?"

Archer stopped pacing and looked out the window toward Serenity. He thought about his young students' eager faces and the way teaching them had brought so much joy back to the game. He thought about Luna, and how she had helped him find himself again.

"I see her." He swallowed hard. "But what if that's not enough? What if I stay, and she continues pushing me away? What if I give up my last chance to stay connected to professional golf?"

"Or what if you take the job and spend the rest of your life wondering what might have been?" Dawson said. "A woman like Luna isn't going to just sit around. Somebody's going to snatch her up."

Archer's phone buzzed—another email from Oakland Hills, asking for a final decision, wanting to make an announcement.

"I need to think," he muttered, walking toward the door.

"Well, don't think too long," Dawson called after him. "Some chances don't come around twice."

"Well, my goodness, you look terrible," Dixie announced as she appeared in Luna's doorway, holding another armful of books. Luna's library was bursting at the seams. "And don't you tell me you're fine, because we both know that's not true."

"Dixie, I don't want to be rude, but I have clients coming."

"Not for another hour," Dixie said, setting down the books. "You want to tell me why you're pushing away the best thing that's happened to you since you came to Seagrove?"

"I'm not pushing him away. I'm setting appropriate boundaries, and goodness gracious, things get around in this town very quickly."

"Boundaries," Dixie scoffed. "Honey, that boy looks at you like you hung the moon, and you look at him the same way when you think nobody's watching."

Luna's composure started to crack. "He's leaving, Dixie. He has this amazing opportunity in California, and I'm not going to be the reason he stays and gives up his dream."

"Did he tell you that?"

"No, he doesn't have to. I heard him talking to Dawson about it."

Dixie was quiet for a moment. "So you decided to make the choice easier by breaking both of your hearts at the same time."

"I'm giving him the freedom to choose without guilt. It's the same thing I told Janine, who I assume told you," Luna said, rolling her eyes.

"Oh, sugar." Dixie moved closer. "Don't you think he deserves to make that choice with all the facts, including how you feel about him?"

"I can't tell him how I feel," Luna said. "It would only make things harder for him."

"Harder than this? Honey, you're not sleeping. You're barely eating. SuAnn says you haven't even been to Hotcakes in days."

"I'm fine."

"You're about as fine as Archer is. You should see him trying to teach those kids. I can tell something's majorly wrong. One of the kids asked why Coach looks so sad."

Luna's chest tightened. She hadn't let herself think about how her withdrawal might affect Archer. She figured he'd get over it quickly, as most of the men in her past had done.

"He'll be fine once he gets to California," she said. The words tasted bitter in her mouth. "He'll have a fresh start and a chance to build something meaningful."

"And what about what he's already built here? Those kids adore him. The whole town respects him. Not only for what he did when he was a professional golfer, but what he does now. And you—"

"Please don't," Luna whispered.

"Well, somebody has to say it. You love him. And from where I'm standing, he loves you, too. That kind of love doesn't come along every day."

Luna found herself wondering if he had accepted the job. The time had passed for when he was supposed to answer. Oakland Hills? Did he tell them yes? Was he leaving soon? Had he already packed the few things he brought with him to Seagrove? She wanted to know. She wanted to ask Dixie if she knew, but she was afraid the answer might just break her heart.

"Sometimes love isn't enough. Haven't you ever heard that before?"

"Only when we don't give it a chance to be enough."

"You don't understand," Luna said, wrapping her arms around her body. "Every time I've opened my heart and tried to build something with someone, it all falls apart. My marriage, my practice in Austin…"

"Is that what this is really about? You're not just protecting Archer from having to choose. You're protecting yourself from feeling left behind again."

She thought about how she really was about to feel left behind if Archer left.

"Look, I came here to help others, Dixie. To create something meaningful. I never expected—"

"Yes, I know. To need healing yourself."

Dixie's bangles clinked as she touched Luna's arm. "Honey, sometimes the best healing happens when we stop trying to control every little thing. When we just let ourselves be vulnerable and let the chips fall where they may."

"I can't." Luna's voice broke. "I can't watch him leave. Not after..."

"After what?"

"After he made me believe in magic again. In second chances. The way he looks at me sometimes, like I'm something precious. Nobody's ever looked at me that way."

"Then why are you pushing that away?"

"Because it will hurt less to end it now on my own terms than watch him choose California over—over me."

"Honey, has it occurred to you that maybe he's waiting for a reason to stay?"

Before Luna could respond, she heard a car door slam outside. Through the window, she saw Archer getting into his truck, his shoulders set in a way she recognized, like he'd made a decision about something.

Her heart clenched. The Oakland Hills deadline was today.

CHAPTER 13

Luna stood at her window, unable to look away as she watched Archer load boxes into his truck outside of Dawson's Inn. She couldn't believe he was leaving. She didn't even get to tell him good-bye, but that was her own fault because she had turned him away when he came over. Her heart felt like it was being squeezed as she watched Julie hug him and then Dawson clap him on the back. He was leaving. He'd made his choice. That was that.

"Maybe he's just moving some things," Janine suggested from behind her. She'd come to their morning yoga session only to find Luna frozen at the window.

"No." Luna's voice was barely above a whisper. "The Oakland Hills deadline passed. He made his decision."

She watched as Archer climbed into his truck. He looked over toward Serenity for a long moment, and Luna stepped away from the window.

"Luna," Janine started.

"I have clients coming," Luna said, sliding on her professional mask once again. "We should cancel yoga this morning. You should be home with Madison anyway. You said she wasn't feeling well."

"Well, I'm not leaving you alone right now."

"I'm fine," Luna said. "This is what I wanted, remember? For him to be free to choose without complications."

"You're not a complication."

The sound of Archer's truck starting cut off Janine's words. Luna fixed her eyes on the desk until the rumble of the engine faded into the distance. He was gone, and she had no one to blame but herself. She didn't even fight for him. She just couldn't. She cared more about his happiness than her own.

She moved through the next few days in a fog, throwing herself into as much work at Serenity as possible. She was almost manic about it, calling up different contractors to fix things that didn't need fixing, adding more classes to her schedule, running into town to put up flyers—anything she could do to keep herself busy. She extended her hours just so she could keep her mind occupied from thinking about Archer leaving.

"You need to rest," Janine said on the third morning. "When was the last time you actually slept?"

"I'm fine," Luna said.

She knew it was a lie. The dark circles under her eyes told a different story.

"You're not fine at all. None of this is fine." Janine crossed her arms. "Do you have a therapist yourself? Have you even let yourself cry this out?"

"There's nothing to cry about, Janine. He made his choice. I'm happy for him. Life goes on."

But life didn't feel like it was going on. Every morning she expected to see his truck in her driveway bringing coffee. Every time the door opened, her heart jumped, thinking maybe he'd come back.

"At least go talk to Julie," Janine said. "Find out how he's—"

"No." Luna's voice was sharp. "I don't want to know how he's doing. I can't. I need to focus on my business, on my clients. They're the reason I came here in the first place."

But Luna couldn't help thinking about how Archer had helped guide her through a golf swing, his breath warm against her ear, and how natural it had been to dance in his arms at the golf classic. He looked at her like she was the most precious thing in the world, something worth staying for—except she hadn't been.

"You at least need some air," Janine said later that afternoon. "Come watch the sunset with me at the lighthouse."

Luna shook her head. "I have client notes to finish."

"You know those notes can wait. You've been cooped up in here for days, drowning yourself in work. Come on, Luna. Just come with me."

Luna finally looked up, and Janine's face was filled with concern.

"Fine," she conceded, "but just for a little while. I really do have these notes."

The walk to the lighthouse was quiet, the early evening air heavy with salt and jasmine.

"I'm sure those kids miss their golf lessons," Janine said as they started to climb the lighthouse steps.

"I'm sure Oakland Hills will have plenty of young students eager to learn from him."

"Luna—"

"Please," Luna interrupted. "I can't talk about him. Not yet."

They reached the top of the lighthouse as the sun began its descent. Luna moved to the railing, letting the wind whip her long hair around her face.

"I need to check on Madison," Janine said suddenly. "William just texted. She's running a fever again."

Luna nodded, not turning around. "Go on, I'll be fine here."

She heard Janine's footsteps fade down the stairs, leaving her alone with the sunset and her thoughts. She closed her eyes, listening to the endless rhythm of the ocean. Right now, peace felt very far away.

She heard footsteps on the stairs behind her and turned, thinking Janine had come right back, but instead, she met Emma, who took care of the light-house and lived on-site. She was very nice and had invited Luna to have lunch one day. Luna was grateful to be meeting new people and to maybe have some distractions in the coming days.

Emma headed back down, and Luna decided to stay a few more minutes until the sun was almost gone before walking home.

Luna closed her eyes again and allowed the sea breeze to blow her hair. This was usually something that calmed her, but right now she couldn't seem to find that peace within herself. All she could think about was watching Archer load up his truck and leave. Had everything meant nothing to him? Did he think that he meant nothing to her? It was all so jumbled up in her brain.

She heard footsteps behind her yet again and thought, *Who in the world would be coming up to the lighthouse at this hour when the sun was almost gone?* Maybe Emma was coming back because she felt bad for her being alone, but what she really wanted was to be alone.

"I've been looking for you."

Luna's heart felt like it stopped in her chest. She thought she'd imagined his voice for a moment, another trick of grief and exhaustion, but when she turned, Archer was standing there, real and solid.

"Archer. I thought you were in California," she managed to choke out.

"I never left." He took a step closer. "I could never do that."

"But I saw you—your truck, the boxes—"

"I moved into my own place in town, a cottage near the golf course." His eyes held hers. "I'm staying, Luna. I turned down Oakland Hills days ago."

She gripped the railing behind her. "But why?"

"Because everything I need is here. Everything I want is here." He took another step closer. "The kids, the community, the chance to continue teaching the game I love in a way that matters. But most of all—you."

She felt tears burning her eyes. "I pushed you away."

"You tried," he said, slightly smiling. "But I learned something from all those breathing exercises you forced me to learn. Sometimes the hardest thing to do is also the most important."

"And what's that?"

"Staying still. Letting yourself feel everything, even when it hurts."

He was close enough now that she could see those little flecks of gold in his eyes.

"I'm done running, Luna. From my injury, from my feelings, and from this thing between us."

Luna felt her carefully constructed walls crumble.

"But I heard you talking to Dawson about Oakland Hills, about making a difference there. And I wasn't going to be the reason you gave that up."

"And you weren't the reason I gave it up," he said. "You were the reason I finally understood what making a difference really means. Those kids on the course, the way they light up when they make a good shot—that's real. You helped me find myself again. I don't need more money. I made plenty as a pro. That job wasn't what I needed."

"Archer—"

"Let me finish." His voice was gentle but urgent.

"I spent my whole life chasing the next big thing, pushing through pain, trying to prove myself to everybody else. And then you taught me how to be still and find joy in small moments. How could I leave that?"

"I was so scared," she whispered, as a tear slipped from her eye and down her cheek. "Of needing you. Of not being enough to make you stay."

"Hey." He reached out, brushing away the tear with his thumb. "You're not just enough. You're everything."

The touch of his hand felt like everything broke loose inside her. All the pain and grief of the last few days crashed over her like a rogue wave threatening to take her down.

"I thought you were gone," she choked out. "I thought I'd lost you without ever telling you—"

"Telling me what?"

Luna met his eyes.

"That I love you."

The words hung in the air between them.

Archer's hand stilled against her cheek.

"Say that again," he whispered.

"I love you. Even when I was pushing you away, even when I thought I had lost you—I loved you."

He moved closer, his free hand finding her waist.

"I love you, too," he said. "More than any game, any job offer, or any dream I ever had before you."

The last of the sunlight painted the lighthouse in gold. Here, where the land met the sea, more endings became beginnings. This was where they were meant to be.

When Archer finally kissed her, it felt like coming home. His lips were gentle against hers, giving her time to respond, asking rather than demanding. She melted into him, her hand sliding up his chest and curling around his neck. They kissed slowly, like the tide coming in.

Archer's arms tightened around her waist, pulling her closer, and she could feel his heartbeat against her own. And when they finally broke apart, Luna kept her eyes closed for a moment, memorizing the feeling.

Archer rested his forehead against hers.

"Stay with me. No more running. No more pushing away. Just stay."

She opened her eyes.

"I'm not going anywhere," she promised.

The wind picked up, and Luna stayed in Archer's arms, feeling the last tension leave her body as he pressed a soft kiss to her temple.

"By the way, you can thank Janine," he said, "and Emma. This wasn't exactly a spontaneous sunset visit. It might have been a setup."

Luna laughed softly.

"I wondered why Emma disappeared so quickly. I met her, and she was gone just as fast."

"I think the whole town's been conspiring to get us here." Archer's thumb traced circles on her lower back. "Dawson has been insufferable about it."

"You mean because he was right? Because they were all right?"

"About us belonging together? About some things

being worth more than career moves or careful plans?"

She reached up to touch his face, tracing the line of his jaw.

"When did you know you wouldn't take the job?"

"The moment I thought about teaching somewhere without hearing you laugh from the deck on Serenity, or standing on the sidelines without seeing your face light up, I realized I didn't want any future that didn't have you in it."

"And what does that future look like?"

"Mornings on the golf course with the kids, evenings watching the sunset from Serenity's deck, you teaching me about breathing and me teaching you about golf, and then the two of us learning other things together. Though you're actually a pretty good golf student."

"Well, I had an excellent teacher," Luna said.

"We make a good team. The therapist and the golf pro."

"Former pro," Luna corrected. "Current miracle worker with kids who never thought they'd love the game."

"You see me so clearly—not who I was, but who I am now and who I want to be."

"And that goes both ways," she said. "You saw past my careful plans and professional boundaries and made me want to risk my heart again."

He leaned down to kiss her again. When he pulled back, the last light of the sunset caught his face.

"We should probably head down," she said, "before somebody sends up a search party."

"Or before Janine starts texting the whole town that her plan worked." Luna laughed.

"Too late for that, I'm sure."

EPILOGUE

L una stood at the edge of the crowd gathered outside the Seagrove Golf Club and watched as Archer cut the ceremonial ribbon for his new Seagrove Junior Golf Academy. She felt so much pride as dozens of young students and their parents, local press, and what seemed like most of the town turned out to celebrate.

"He looks so happy," Janine whispered, bouncing her daughter in her arms. Madison cooed softly, reaching for the colorful ribbon floating in the breeze.

"He is very happy," Luna said as she watched Archer shake hands with the club president.

The past six months had transformed him. He was no longer that angry, injured athlete who'd first walked into Serenity. In his place stood a man who had finally found his true calling.

"You know, a magazine in Charleston wants to do a whole spread on him," Julie said, walking up beside them with her camera. "They're calling it *From Pro Tour to Prodigy Maker*. The reporter's coming next week."

"Look at my boy," SuAnn beamed. "Though I still say he needs to eat more. These early morning lessons are probably running him ragged."

"The early morning lessons are his favorite part of the day," Luna said, laughing.

Dixie adjusted her flowing pink dress, her bangles jingling as usual. "Well, my favorite part is watching him and Luna do that sunset yoga on the beach. They look like a power couple."

"Speaking of power couples," Dawson said, "wait until you see what Archer's done with the academy curriculum. He's incorporated Luna's breathing techniques into every lesson."

Luna smiled, remembering how they had worked on those together. Serenity's morning classes included golfers working on their mental game, while Archer's students learned about mindfulness alongside their swing mechanics.

"The waiting list for lessons is three months long," Julie said. "People are driving from Savannah and Charleston just to work with him."

Archer caught Luna's eye across the crowd, his face softening into a smile that he always reserved just for her. He excused himself from the parents and made his way over.

"Well, there's my favorite therapist," he said, slipping his arm around her waist. "Ready for the tour?"

The new academy space was everything he'd envisioned, a perfect blend of traditional golf instruction and some modern holistic space. Large windows overlooked the practice green.

"Oakland Hills called again last week," he said as they stood in his new office, "offered me double their original offer."

"And of course, I told them I'm exactly where I want to be." He pulled her closer. "Where I *need* to be."

Luna leaned into his embrace, taking in the view from his office window. Young students were already gathering on the practice green, clubs in hand.

"You've built something special here," she said softly.

"We both have." He pressed a kiss to her temple. "You know, Serenity's waitlist is just as long as mine. Though I hear some people are signing up just to watch a handsome golf coach do his morning breathing exercises on the deck."

Luna laughed. "Yeah, that's what Dixie's claiming anyway."

"Well, we can't disappoint Dixie. She's telling everyone who comes into the bookstore that she predicted the whole thing."

"Oh, did she now?"

"Oh, yes. According to her, she knew from the moment she saw me lurking around outside Serenity."

"She wasn't wrong."

They made their way back to the celebration, where SuAnn was setting up a spread that would feed half of Seagrove. Madison was asleep in Janine's arms, and Julie was snapping photos.

"You know, sometimes I think about that first movement class and how terrified I was to admit that I needed help."

"And now look at you, teaching kids that it's okay to take things slowly and to breathe when there's hard stuff."

"Well, I had the best teacher," he said, squeezing her hand.

"Time for a toast!" Dixie called out, gathering everyone around. "To Archer and his junior golf academy—proof that sometimes life's little detours lead us to exactly where we're supposed to be."

"And to Luna," Archer said, raising his glass, "who

taught me that healing isn't just about fixing what's broken, but about discovering what's possible."

Six months ago, she couldn't have imagined this moment—Archer thriving in his new role and Serenity becoming an integral part of the community.

"Well, I knew that night at the lighthouse that things would work out," Emma said, walking up behind them.

"Did everyone in town conspire to get us together?" Luna asked, laughing.

"Honey, we just provided the opportunities," SuAnn interjected. "You two did all the hard work yourselves."

This was their life now—morning breathing on Serenity's deck, afternoon lessons at the academy, sunset walks on the beach. And Luna realized this was the greatest healing of all.

When the celebration wound down, they walked hand in hand along the beach toward Serenity.

"Remember our first golf lesson?" Archer said, pulling her close. "When you told me sometimes the hardest thing is learning to be still?"

"Yes. And now you're teaching that to others."

"Well, we both are." He stopped walking, turning to face her. "You know, I used to think losing my career was the worst thing that could happen to me.

But if I hadn't gotten injured and hadn't come back to Seagrove—"

"You wouldn't be changing lives," Luna suggested.

"No." He shook his head. "I wouldn't have found *you*," he corrected. "Wouldn't have learned that sometimes life's greatest gifts come disguised as setbacks."

"Well, we took the scenic route," she said, "but we got here."

His kiss was gentle but familiar, and no less magical than the first one at the lighthouse.

"Here," he agreed, "is exactly where we're meant to be."

Ownload your FREE Seagrove welcome packet by clicking this image or typing the link below. You'll get a bonus scene, recipes from

Seagrove, adult coloring sheets, printable book-marks & more!

G et it here: https://BookHip.com/LCKQZDK

D id you know I have a private Facebook reader group with over 20,000 members? We have a ton of fun in there every day, so if you'd like to engage with me personally and meet other great people, join us here: https://www.facebook.com/groups/RachelReaders